# The Tears of Buddha

## A Montclaire Mystery

# E.A. Allen

# The Tears of Buddha

Being a Record of the Horrible Murder
of Marie-Claire Bernard and
The Remarkable Events That Followed

From the Journals of Colonel Sir Francis FitzMaurice

Addison & Highsmith

# Addison & Highsmith Publishers

Las Vegas ◊ Chicago ◊ Palm Beach

Published in the United States of America by
Histria Books, a division of Histria LLC
7181 N. Hualapai Way, Ste. 130-86
Las Vegas, NV 89166 USA
HistriaBooks.com

Addison & Highsmith is an imprint of Histria Books. Titles published under the imprints of Histria Books are distributed worldwide.

Library of Congress Control Number: 2022940454

ISBN 978-1-59211-175-6 (hardcover)
ISBN 978-1-59211-371-2 (softbound)
ISBN 978-1-59211-243-2 (eBook)

# Contents

*We should forgive our enemies, but not before they are hanged.*

— Heinrich Heine

# An Editor's Foreword

*It is said that about the year 765, during the reign of Li Yu, The Daizong Emperor of the Tang Dynasty, in the far western Buddhist Monastery of Wenshu, the potter Bai Fu fashioned a group of three identical bowls, in the new tricolor style of porcelain making. The monks of Wenshu found the bowls so perfect in their simplicity of style and form that they presented them to the monastery's great temple statue of Buddha. It is said further that as the monks prayed their offering the Buddha's statue began to weep and three tears descended upon its cheek. Thereafter, the three bowls were prized by the monks and later by Emperors of the Tang, and they were called The Tears of Buddha.*

# Prologue
# Madame Courbon Hears a Noise

*Paris, November 1907*

"What!" she gasped, jolting from a sound sleep and sitting bolt upright in her bed. "What is it?" Groggy, confused, and at first unaware of what had awakened her, Madame Courbon groped in the darkness at her bedside table, searching for a match to light her lamp. Now, listening intently, there came from somewhere above a noise of furniture crashing and of a door banging, and as quickly as it had begun, the noise stopped. Next, she heard the shuffle of feet on the stairs, and then silence. A frightening silence.

A concierge is duty-bound to ensure good order in her building. Such noises in the night demanded investigation. Madame Courbon dressed hurriedly, not bothering to remove her kerchief. Holding a small lamp, she opened her door a crack and peered out to the stairs. All quiet. She climbed slowly, warily to the upper story where the noises had come from; listening for any sound that might signal danger. All was still quiet.

There were two doors to apartments on that level. The door to one was slightly ajar. She pushed it reluctantly, holding high her lamp to see inside. Even in the dark, she could see overturned furniture.

Fearing an intruder might still lurk inside, she considered retreating, but duty required an investigation, so she pushed the door wide and strained to see inside. It was then she saw it. There on the floor of the sitting room. The horror of it caused her to scream and then to run out to the stairs and down, shrieking all the while. When she reached the Rue des Vignes, she shrieked all the louder, hoping to rouse the gendarme who walked the neighborhood at night. She had forgotten her whistle on the table by her bed, so she could only shriek and scream for him.

Finally, after what seemed like hours but was only a few minutes, the policeman rounded the corner from Rue Pajou, and by the glow of the gaslight at the corner, ran to Madame Courbon. By then her shouting had roused the neighbors, who threw open their windows and peered down into the street, curious to see what the matter was.

"What is it, Madame," the gendarme asked, breathless. Pointing to the open portal of her building she gasped, "There. Go there."

Not waiting for further explanation the gendarme entered, with Madame Courbon close behind. "Up there," she urged, still holding her lamp. "The second level."

When they arrived, the door lay open. Taking the lamp from Madame, the policeman entered, turning up the wick as he went.

It lay on the floor, now fully visible. The body of a woman lay in the middle of the room, her head a mass of blood. Here and there blood had splashed on the floor and on the wall, where there was also the bloody print of a hand. A small hand. Madame drew a deep breath at the ghastly mess. Even the gendarme recoiled in horror to see it and then retched.

As the policeman found a lamp in the room and turned it up to the full flame, his heart stopped to hear a noise from behind the large chair to one side. "Come out!" he ordered, thinking it must be the murderer. Nothing. "Come out, I say!" Still no response. Finally, as he and Madame Courbon prepared to look behind the chair, out crawled a baby, her clothing soaked in blood. The little girl crawled over to the corpse and there, began to tug at the victim's arm and to plead — "Maman... Maman... Maman."

Madame Courbon began to cry.

# PART ONE
## Tang Bowls and Tragedy

# Chapter One
## "Wake Up!"

"Fitz," I heard Montclaire's raspy voice at my door. "Fitz!" he repeated. "Wake up!"

I reached for my watch on the table beside my bed and then turned up the lamp. Confused, eyes half-open and sensitive to light, I could make out that it was just short of three o'clock. My first thought was that no good can come of a chap being awakened at three o'clock and entirely against his will. No good at all.

As I sat up and searched for my robe, I heard voices — the sound of frantic conversation. Just outside my door, I came face-to-face with Petrovsky — Montclaire's Russian manservant — still in his nightshirt. Odd, I never thought of Petrovsky in a nightshirt. I'd always imagined that Cossacks slept in bearskins or some such primitive costume. Coming face-to-face with Petrovsky at that hour of the morning was bound to startle. His bushy black beard and large, flat nose... well, he had the sort of face that causes people of a charitable disposition to say when they see it, "Let us hope for the best."

"Petrovsky, what is it?" I finally managed to ask.

"There, Sir Francis," he said, pointing toward the library. "They're in there."

When I opened the doors I first saw Montclaire, also in his robe, and then young Etienne Picot, the open-faced Sûreté detective who had become Montclaire's protégé.

I don't know why but the first thing that struck me was that Montclaire's jet-black hair was perfectly coiffed and his cold blue eyes, perfectly alert — two things that seemed out of place at that hour.

"What is it?" I asked, knowing that only a tragedy could have brought Picot to our door at that hour.

"Picot here was just about to tell me, Fitz. You've arrived just in time to hear it too," said Montclaire, drawing a cigarette from his case and lighting it with a firebrand from the hearth. "Please continue, Picot," he said, taking a chair by the fire. Picot and I did the same.

"The Minister sent me, Monsieur," he said breathlessly.

That made me sit up. French Ministers don't usually roam about ordering the Sûreté here and there in the middle of the night.

"Ah, how is your uncle, Picot?" Montclaire asked in his nonchalant way. "And what is it that disturbs old Brouillard's sleep? Poor fellow." Just then Petrovsky arrived with coffee all round.

"He is almost apoplectic, Monsieur," said Picot, a sigh in his voice. Montclaire tossed me a questioning glance.

"He was summoned from his bed at midnight, as I was also, and he has sent me to fetch you to the Rue des Vignes. There, I can assure you, you will find the most horrible scene of a murder that you have ever beheld, Monsieur. The Minister summons you to see it, undoubtedly because he wishes you to undertake an investigation."

"But, Picot. Why me? You and the Sûreté are surely capable of investigating a murder. Sadly, Paris is full of murders."

"This is no ordinary murder, as you can well imagine, or else the Minister would not insist upon you. It's only my speculation, but I assume he wishes you to act as Examining Magistrate."

Montclaire's head dropped, in resignation I thought. I knew his reluctance to become involved in any investigation at the moment. We'd just returned from London, exhausted by that sordid affair concerning the French Ambassador's promiscuous daughter.

"Very well, Picot," he finally said. "Sir Francis and I will join you in your coach as soon as we can dress."

# Chapter Two
# Picot Explains

Once in the coach and moving south through empty streets, Picot explained.

"The victim is a young woman — a young widow, named Marie-Claire Bernard. She'd been stabbed several times and her throat cut. A bloody mess." Picot shook his head.

"And how did she come to be discovered?" Montclaire asked.

"The concierge. A woman named Madame Courbon. Heard 'something' in the night and decided to investigate. Found the door ajar. Saw what was inside. Ran into the street screaming like a lost soul."

Montclaire leaned back and looked briefly out the window.

"How is it you've come to me, Picot? You say the Minister sent you?"

"Oui." Said Picot, pausing to gather his thoughts. "Marie-Claire Bernard is no ordinary victim, as it turns out. She is the widow of a military hero of North Africa fame — Charles Bernard…."

"Oh yes!" I interrupted. "Captain Bernard. The chap who was killed in that dust-up in Algiers last year. A hero indeed. Said so in all the papers, as I recall."

"Oui, Sir Francis. But there's more. Marie-Claire Bernard is also a daughter of the Joffre family — a very wealthy clan who as you may know have made their fortune in banking and such," Picot continued.

"Yes," Montclaire acknowledged, "and politically powerful as well, which is why the Minister is so interested, eh?"

"Exactly," Picot confirmed, "and not just politically important, but very influential with the Nationalists, who the Government is particularly eager to placate at the moment."

Montclaire's eyes narrowed. "But surely the murder was motivated by ordinary villainy of some kind — theft or perhaps *un crime passionnel.*

"You say the concierge heard a noise. What sort of noise?" Montclaire probed.

"She's not sure. Just a noise that was loud enough to rouse her from a sound sleep, and from a floor away. Then, she says she heard the shuffle of feet on the stairs, and that was when she decided to rise and investigate."

"Aside from the body, did the gendarme find anything else in the apartment?

Picot paused. "Oui, Monsieur. He found the victim's daughter. A baby of two years. Apparently, the child was...." He paused.

"Was what?" I almost hesitated to ask, fearing the worst.

"She was crawling about the floor, with her clothing soaked in her mother's blood."

Picot closed his eyes. The image he described made me gasp. Montclaire's mouth opened a tad and then he made one of those little noises French people make that have no equivalent in English. I recognized this one as a combination of surprise and sympathy, and then his eyes grew cold.

# Chapter Three
## Bloody Murder and Art

As we descended from Picot's coach at 12 rue des Vignes, I glimpsed a considerable crowd of gawkers, observing from across the street. The gendarmes were busy keeping them away from the front of the building. Picot guided us up the stairs and directly to the victim's door. Though we were forewarned, our first glance inside was horrifying.

A gaggle of gendarmes lolled about the sitting room, where the body still lay, now covered by a bloody sheet. Splattering and smears of blood-covered one wall and the room had been ransacked. Books had been thrown from the shelves and, at one corner, a writing desk had been torn to pieces and lay scattered on the floor. From another room, we could hear the sound of a child crying and occasionally whining "*Maman.*" *En semble*, it was ghastly.

Montclaire paid little attention to the mess but immediately began to glance about the room. Soon, he knelt beside the body and lifted the sheet, to reveal the true horror of what had happened. The young woman's glazed eyes were open wide in the horror of her last moments of life and her head was almost severed. She'd been stabbed, hacked, and sliced. *Butchery* was the word that came to mind. I closed my eyes.

When I opened them again, I could see that the woman's clothing had been torn away and it appeared at first glance that she'd been violated.

Looking up, Montclaire asked Picot, coldly.

"Have you found the knife?"

"No."

"Took it away with him, eh?"

"It would seem so."

Montclaire covered the body back up and ordered the waiting men from the Paris Morgue to remove Marie-Claire. "Release the body to her family," he ordered, "but only after a full examination. Tell the director, eh? And see if he can confirm that the young woman was raped."

At first Montclaire looked about the room in his way, examining everything closely. He seemed to find nothing of interest. Then he went into other parts of the house, stopping in the kitchen. There he found a large towel, clearly with blood on it, beside the water bowl. He picked up the towel, examined it carefully, and then returned it to the cabinet.

"The murderer wiped his hands and face and even wiped his knife."

Then, as if an afterthought, he picked up the towel again and held it to his nose. Still holding it to his nose, he said more to himself than to me, "Wiped the blood from his face too. Left the smell of his eau de cologne. An inferior scent called Hoyt's. Made in Germany, but available at a modest price in France too."

*There's a man with a nose for crime*, I thought to myself when suddenly I heard sounds of a ruckus outside on the landing. When the door opened, two gendarmes entered, holding fast by each elbow a pink little man with a bald head, red nose, and bushy eyebrows.

"Monsieur!" he pleaded at Montclaire as we reentered the setting-room. "Monsieur!"

"Who the devil are you and what's your business here?" Montclaire demanded. "Release him," he told the gendarmes. Indignant, the little man straightened his cravat and suitcoat and then stood upright, his chin defiant.

"Edouard Dulac, Monsieur," he said with a sense of importance, as he took from his waistcoat a card and handed it to Montclaire.

"You are a 'Dealer in Fine Art,' it says." What business have you here?" Montclaire asked, still thumbing the card.

Monsieur Dulac glanced about the room and then gasped to see the bloody sheet on the floor. He fell back and when he swooned a little, Picot took his arm.

"Is that…?" he asked, his eyes fearful.

"Never mind who that is, Monsieur Dulac. Again, what is your business here?" Montclaire demanded, this time with an angry tone in his voice.

Dulac stood to his full height, which was not very much, and answered, "I am here, Monsieur, to see Madame Bernard, on a matter of business."

"I am Gérard de Montclaire and I am here leading an investigation of murder, Monsieur Dulac." Dulac recognized the name and it seemed to unsettle him. He quickly regained his composure, as Montclaire continued.

"What business precisely was it that you had with Mme. Bernard, Monsieur?"

Dulac hesitated to answer, but faced with what was going on around him, he quickly relented.

"I had an appointment with Madame Bernard this morning to discuss the purchase of some *objet d'art*."

Montclaire's eyebrows lifted a little. "Come, Dulac. Do not hold back. There is no use to be reticent."

"We were to discuss the sale of three bowls, Monsieur, belonging to Madame's family. The Joffre. Her father, Monsieur Pierre Joffre is a well-known financier, eh?"

"Yes, I know. And…?"

"I was told the family wished to sell the bowls, which have been in their possession for many years, but that the sale was to be very discreet. That's why Mme. Bernard was the go-between."

"You were here to discuss price then?"

"No. We'd already agreed upon a price, and I delivered my advance of payment to Madame two days ago. I was here this morning to present my cheque and to take possession of the bowls."

"What sort of bowls?" Montclaire asked.

"Three identical bowls, each about nine centimeters in diameter. They are Chinese in origin."

Montclaire turned to the policeman who was heading the detail of gendarmes. "Have you found three bowls fitting that description?"

"No, sir."

Montclaire turned to Dulac. "Monsieur Dulac, if you please."

"Of course."

"This is an odd time of day to make a call to purchase art. It's nearly six o'clock."

The little man paused. "*Bien, Monsieur.* The sale was a delicate matter with Madame Bernard and her family. Er... she did not say so precisely, but I was given to understand that financial considerations required them to part with the bowls. And so, she insisted that I come at a time of day when no one would be likely to observe if you know what I mean."

"Quite," said Montclaire, raising his chin a bit.

"Have you, for your part, told anyone about the presence of the bowls, here in this apartment. Anyone?"

Dulac rocked back a little at the directness of the question.

"Oh, no, Monsieur. No one. The Joffres were particularly concerned that I should keep the transaction in strictest confidence."

"These bowls... quite valuable, I presume?" I asked.

"Oh yes. They are almost priceless. They are a rare treasure of the Tang Dynasty, Monsieur. There is no prize of Chinese porcelain more coveted than *The Tears of Buddha*."

"The what?" I blurted.

"The bowls, Monsieur. In the world of Chinese porcelain, they are called by the name that has been attached to them since the eighth century. They are called *The Tears of Buddha*."

"Monsieur Dulac, you may wait here while we make a thorough search of the apartment. I was about to order that as you arrived."

Guided by a gendarme, Dulac took a seat in the corner of the ransacked room, and there he sat almost motionless and without expression as we, Picot, and four gendarmes began a painstaking search of Marie-Claire's rooms.

"I particularly wish you to collect anything that is written," Montclaire instructed, and particularly anything that looks like a journal or diary the victim might have kept. Then, I want you to search every inch of the floors, walls, and ceiling of this apartment for a secret compartment big enough to hide three small Chinese bowls."

Just then the men from the Paris Morgue hoisted the body, still covered in its bloody sheet, onto their stretcher and strained to carry it out the door and down the stairs to their waiting ambulance. Somehow, we could not avert our eyes as they did so.

While the gendarmes went methodically about their searching, Montclaire turned again to the glum art dealer, sitting in the corner.

"Monsieur Dulac. You say the bowls are priceless. Surely not, if you were to buy them. How much had you agreed to pay for them?"

Dulac paused. "We'd agreed upon a sum of 20 million French Francs, Monsieur, and I considered that I had gotten a bargain."

"Good Heavens!" I could not help blurting. "That's a king's ransom."

"'Tis more than a king's ransom, Monsieur," Dulac advised. "No one would pay as much for a mere king."

Montclaire smiled gently. "I dare say. In our time, the value of kings is waning. And, I suppose the value of rare bowls is increasing."

"Precisely," Dulac agreed. "And now perhaps their cost includes the murder of that unfortunate woman." He sighed.

# Chapter Four
# A Grieving Family

Montclaire released Dulac, who fled the building like it was on fire. We remained in the apartment most of the morning, superintending the search. Picot brought in additional gendarmes to help and by noon everything had been examined. There was little of the paper records Montclaire had demanded and no hidden compartment for valuables. No diary.

"Women of a certain class and especially young women often keep a journal, and so I find it interesting that Marie-Claire's journal, if she had one, is not here," Montclaire explained to Picot.

"Perhaps it is the usual thing, Monsieur," Picot allowed, "but some women do not. It may well be that Marie-Claire was one of those, eh?"

Montclaire shrugged in his Gallic way and continued to thumb through the papers that we'd found.

"A few letters. Receipts for various purchases. Some notes about cooking. Papers concerning her daughter, including the baby's baptismal certificate. Much the usual sort of thing one would find," Montclaire frowned, as he handed the bundle to Picot. "See that these are all retained in the file of this case."

"Oui, Monsieur."

As Picot turned to leave, the Minister arrived, in a huff. Jean-Luc Brouillard was a notoriously grumpy man, but the death of Marie-Claire Bernard, together with a bit of sleeplessness, had accentuated his usual malaise. A small lean man in his middle years, Brouillard's balding head and slender face featured a large Gallic nose. The lip beneath the nose was festooned with a substantial mustache, which seemed to function as a cushion for the nose. In the ten years that I had known Brouillard, he always had a look on his face like a man who was preparing to tell you about his great secret sorrow.

"Montclaire, you must accept my commission as Examining Magistrate in this affair. This matter is far too sensitive to leave to the ordinary run of prosecutor," he huffed, drawing a document from his inside coat pocket and handing it to Montclaire.

"Seems in order, Minister," Montclaire said, reading the paper, "and I accept your commission." With that last, he took a pen from Picot, signed, and returned the document to Brouillard.

"And now you must confide in me all that you know of the sensitivities of this affair. Why do you require me?"

Brouillard paused a moment to collect his thoughts — or wits — and then explained. "You undoubtedly know that the dead woman is the daughter of Pierre Joffre, the financier. Bien, this Joffre is also politically influential, but that is not the reason for your presence. Just between ourselves, Montclaire, the Government suspects that Joffre — who is a Nationalist — is collaborating with foreign business entities to make investments in Persia, in the newly discovered oil lands there. These investments are supported by a foreign government."

"Who?" Montclaire asked, pointedly.

Brouillard paused. "I suppose you must know. After all, I have dragged you into this business. Some evidence points to the Austrians, but... well, you know that the Austrians are not free actors. If they do anything, it is for the benefit of the Kaiser."

Montclaire's eyebrows raised about a quarter inch at the mention of his old enemy.

"So, you suspect Joffre — the dead woman's father — of being in league with German investors in Persia."

"We are not sure, and some even believe he may be allied with American interests," Brouillard responded, "but we suspect."

Montclaire leaned back into a long silence, during which he was digesting all we'd heard. While we waited, Brouillard continued to frown, snort occasionally, and look at his hands, which he was wringing.

"I am not aware that that would be illegal, Minister, even if it were true."

"No, it is not, but it is very unhelpful to France, and it is particularly annoying to our new allies, the English. And they seem to find special annoyance in Joffre's affairs," he added, looking at me.

"How's that?" I asked.

"English companies are competing with others to exploit Persia's petroleum resources, and they are irritated by the likes of Joffre."

"And so you suspect that these financial affairs might have something to do with Marie-Claire's murder?" Montclaire asked.

Brouillard hesitated. "Quite frankly, Montclaire, we don't know what to suspect from them. I merely wished to apprise you of all the equities that could be at play here. That is all. You make your own conclusions, based on your investigation. Just be warned. There is much more here than meets the eye," he advised, narrowing his eyes and nodding in a knowing way.

The next morning, after a restless sleep, I strained to imagine where Montclaire would begin to fathom all the strange issues that seemed to swirl around Marie-Claire's terrible murder. It seemed clear to me that the killer had wanted the valuable bowls, but then decided to add to his villainy by violating his victim.

Soon, Montclaire announced that Picot had called on the telephone device to say that we had an appointment to interview the Joffre family, just after mid-day. Their chateau, just southwest of Paris and near the village of Le Chesnay, would require only a short time to reach.

During that drive, we learned from Picot that the Sûreté had been fast at work investigating Dulac's intimation that the Joffre family were indeed in some financial difficulties. While the young detective did not go into the details of their sources, he related that that seemed to be the case and that it was possible to document that old Joffre had recently borrowed up to his eyebrows from the bankers and had sustained some significant losses is stocks upon the Bourse. All to invest in the Persian oil concessions, many supposed. Montclaire pursed his lips and listened intently to all that Picot reported, without comment.

Finally, he asked, "Is there any reporting from your sources that Joffre is indebted to foreign banks or other institutions?"

"Our banking sources say he is mainly into debt with Lazard Frères and the Rothschild Banking interest. There is one oddity, however. He is involved with an American banker named Morgan, J.P. Morgan."

Montclaire raised an interested eyebrow and leaned back in his seat.

"For another thing," said Picot, opening his notebook to another page.

"What?" I asked as Montclaire came forward in his seat.

"The Joffre's have a son, Georges. By all accounts, he's a wastrel of the first order. Constantly in difficulties of the sort that rich young men encounter, and he is especially said to be deeply in debt to the bookmakers. He is known to be a passionate gambler and has debts littered across Paris."

We drove in a thoughtful silence for a while, and then I noticed Picot's face darken.

"One last thing, Monsieur."

"Yes."

"The director of the Paris Morgue has rendered his report," said the young detective, opening a dossier.

"And?" Montclaire invited.

"He gives the cause of death as 'loss of blood, due to knife wounds,' which is not surprising."

Picot started to continue but then paused.

"There's more?" I asked.

"*Oui*. The director says he cannot be certain, but it appears Marie-Claire had been raped."


After digesting all that Picot said during the long silence that followed, Montclaire posed an unexpected question.

"How is it, Picot, that we find Marie-Claire, the daughter of a very wealthy family, living in... well, in very ordinary circumstances? Her apartment is hardly luxurious and though she had a single maid, that is far fewer servants than a daughter of great wealth would enjoy."

"*Oui*, I have noticed that as well, and I made some inquiries."

"What have you learned?"

"Only this. Apart from the fact that her father might be in some financial distress and therefore unable to support his daughter in style, Marie-Claire insisted on living upon her own resources."

Montclaire thought for a moment and then only said, "An admirable thing if that is as far as it goes."

As is often the case, I was left to wonder what he meant by that and I could tell from Picot's face that he too was a little puzzled.


We found the women of the Joffre family in deep mourning at the loss of their daughter and sister. Madame and her eldest daughter, Sophie, greeted us in the salon. At first, Pierre and his son Georges were nowhere to be seen, but they soon joined us. Pierre — a grizzled little squirt with brooding eyes and side-whiskers — seemed angry, rather than sad. Georges, the young Gawd-help-us of Picot's description, walked with a cane and had a withered foot.

"Have ye found m'bowls, Montclaire?" the old man asked, in a tone both angry and heartless. Made me cringe like a salted slug. "Where are they?" he demanded. "Have ye come to tell me you've caught the filthy bastard who took'em?"

The old buster then fell into a nearby chair, apparently exhausted by the emotions surrounding the loss of his bowls.

"We are eager to do what we can to bring the vicious murderer to justice, Monsieur," said Montclaire, as Madame Joffre stepped forward and bade us take our seats. It was she who spoke next, as Sophie sobbed at her side.

"A pity you did not arrive a bit earlier, Monsieur. Marie-Claire's fiancé — François — was just here. Major François Gargal, that is. He is devastated, of course, as we all are." She fell to tears and seemed to me to be as inconsolable as Sophie.

"*Oui*, a pity" Montclaire agreed. "I had not known your daughter was betrothed." He looked at Picot as if to ask why the Sûreté was not aware of this fact. "But I am certain to meet Major Gargal at a later time."

Not lingering on the missing fiancé, Montclaire got quickly to the point.

"Monsieur Joffre, ladies, can you think of any reason Marie-Claire might have been singled out for such a terrible thing? Any reason?"

"We have asked ourselves that a hundred times, Monsieur, but I can think of nothing, except perhaps...."

Madame Joffre stopped herself in mid-sentence to look at Sophie. Sophie touched her forearm as if to encourage her.

"...except perhaps the Tang bowls."

This was old Joffre's signal to revive. "You find m'bowls, Montclaire, and you'll find the killer! I've heard of you. They say you're clever. Well, use your cleverness to recover m'bowls, eh."

There was much about Monsieur Joffre's manner to dislike, but it was the old bounder's habit of squinting while licking his lips nervously that set me on edge.

"*Oui,*" said Montclaire, "we have already spoken briefly with Monsieur Dulac, who explained to us the business you had with him."

"Marie-Claire took the bowls from here several days ago and was to hand them over to Dulac, who had already put down an advance. Then he, for his part, was to transfer the remainder of the sale price," said Madame Joffre.

"Then that must be the explanation," said Sophie, with conviction. "A theft, which Marie-Claire bravely attempted to prevent. That was like her. To fight back. She was a brave woman."

"*Oui,*" Montclaire agreed, "and that raises the question of who knew Marie-Claire had the bowls in her possession."

The family members looked at each other, and then Pierre answered.

"We knew, of course, and Monsieur Dulac. No one else, to my knowledge." The others nodded their agreement. I looked at Georges, who was not nodding but seemed confused.

"Of course, there's that oily little man, Dulac. Who can know what scoundrels he might have told? He told someone and they murdered Marie-Claire for the bowls. That's what I think," Pierre added.

Montclaire listened with an expressionless face.

"Aye, that's it. Dulac let it out. Show him the whip and he'll tell what he knows, eh?" the old man continued.

By this time I was curious about how old Joffre had learned that his dashed bowls were missing. I knew that Montclaire was probably asking himself the same question.

All the while Joffre spoke, Montclaire nodded agreeably and then changed the subject.

"Did Marie-Claire keep a diary?"

The subject of Marie-Claire's diary did not interest old Joffre at all. He snorted and let out a scoff or two and then rose and toddled out of the room, with Georges on his heels.

"Marie-Claire's death has been an unbearable strain on my husband, Monsieur," said Madame Joffre, as the door closed. "You must forgive him if he does not observe the formalities."

Montclaire nodded and then continued.

"Was there a diary?"

Madame and Sophie looked at each other briefly, apparently not knowing what to answer, but then Sophie spoke, hesitation in her voice.

"I'm not sure, Monsieur, but I believe she did. At least, she kept one several years ago, when she lived at home, and so I suppose she continued."

By this time it was clear that our visit was an undue strain upon a grieving family. We took our leave quickly with more expressions of sympathy to all and with Picot's assurance that the Sûreté would do all in its power to bring the murderer to justice. In the coach, as we left the long drive to the chateau, Picot observed, "That was a grim spectacle, and what did we learn from it?"

I was prepared to lament that we'd learned almost nothing, except perhaps that old Joffre was eager to have his bowls.

Montclaire spoke, looking at Picot. "Yes, and of course, it would be interesting to know how Pierre Joffre knew his bowls are missing."

Picot shrugged. "I would guess someone in the Government, who was privy to my first report of things told him. Or, perhaps Dulac? He probably wants Joffre to return his front money, now that he's unlikely to get the bowls."

There followed a long silence, after which Montclaire returned to a familiar theme.

"It seems that Marie-Claire kept a diary, which we did not find at her apartment. If so, then the murderer took that as well as the bowls."

"What does that signify?" I asked.

"That perhaps Marie-Claire was killed because of something she knew. Something she might have confided to her diary."

After a moment's pause, he continued.

"Bien, we have also learned that the family attributes this tragedy to the theft of the bowls, which seems the most likely motive. But…." He stopped himself, I supposed to reconsider what he was thinking.

"…are we justified — by what we know — to assume that the murderer and whoever took the bowls was one in the same person?"

Picot and I looked at each other.

"If that is so, then you are suggesting we must entertain the possibility that there are two crimes here — and two criminals. Not just one," I followed.

"Yes. Exactly."

That left my head spinning a little, mainly because I found it just a little preposterous.

Picot chose that moment to add to my confusion.

"Georges Joffre is a drug addict, of course, in addition to his other suspected deficiencies. At least, we know that."

"Oui," said Montclaire. "I noticed that as well."

I hadn't noticed any such thing, and so — after yet another brief struggle with being flummoxed — I dared to ask, "How on earth do you chaps know that?" Picot rose to my question.

"It is the nose and eyes, Sir Francis. A certain moist beleaguered look about the eye and a slight sniffle. The badge of the opium-eater, eh."

"Good Heavens! I always took such things to be the sure sign that some poor blighter's been out on an epic toot. See it all the time among fellows at the Albion Club."

Montclaire dropped me a sympathetic smile, while Picot mostly looked at his shoes. And yet, as surprised as I was to learn of young Joffre's opium use and even considering the surprises connected with all we'd heard from Dulac about the bowls, I was yet unprepared for what we were about to learn next day.

Almost breathless, Picot appeared at our door just after breakfast, with a wide-eyed look of distress on his face and a copy of the morning *Figaro* in his hand.

"What is it, Picot?" Montclaire demanded, seeing that something was amiss.

"It's Georges Joffre, Monsieur," he gasped, holding up the newspaper. "Here, Monsieur. Here. At the bottom of the front page," he pointed.

Montclaire took the offered newspaper and read quickly. I could see it was a short article — a notice, merely, but the headline said all one needed to know.

***Georges Joffre kidnapped.***
***Son of financier and brother of recently slain***
***Marie-Claire Bernard.***

# PART TWO

## Spies, Thieves, and Gamblers

# Chapter Five
# A Secret Life

To my surprise, Montclaire showed only a casual interest in young Joffre's kidnapping. Instead of bending all effort to find him, and those who'd taken him, he turned instead to his blasted academic work, preferring, I supposed, to let things percolate. I did not see him all day.

I wanted to encourage Montclaire to act, but I knew from long experience to trust his instinct in such matters. Instead of fretting about the investigation, I repaired to the Albion Club de Paris, where a group of the chaps were organizing a day out at Auteuil, where the racing season was already well underway. There, I put what was left of my monthly money — my *chemisier* you might say — on a filly named Mlle. Picardie, ridden by the great jockey "George" Parfremont. The horse started at very short odds, but I had an ante-post bet on a longshot nag named Suzanne Rouge to place, and when she came in, my winnings doubled, much to the lasting acclaim of my chums, all of whom went home with furrowed brows and empty pockets.

Just after breakfast the next morning, as I was still basking in the warm afterglow of my stunning achievement at Auteuil, Petrovsky announced Etienne Picot. I was not at all surprised to see the young detective, but I am sure my mouth fell open about an inch to see who had accompanied him. I could see that Montclaire was also puzzled, for the companion was none other than Colonel Alexandre Fleury, the head of France's Secret Foreign Intelligence Service — the Deuxième Bureau. Fleury's face was drawn and anxious.

Montclaire's surprise quickly faded, as he offered our visitors a seat by the fire. Petrovsky had anticipated the need for coffee, and as we sat and sipped, Montclaire invited an explanation.

"What brings you to my door, Alexandre? An invitation to do a bit of fencing? It has been far too long since we touched blades."

"An excellent idea, Montclaire, but I am here on a far more serious matter." He looked at Picot, as if for agreement. Picot spoke next.

"I have asked Colonel Fleury to accompany me today, Monsieur, because he is best capable of answering the questions you will surely have when we explain more of what you must know."

"Oh?" Montclaire questioned. "What then, Picot. I am your captive listener."

"Marie-Claire Bernard was no ordinary widow and no mere daughter of privilege."

I perked up to hear that.

"Non," Fleury took up the explanation. "She was also a very talented young woman. In her scholarship, she was a brilliant mathematician... and...."

Fleury looked at us with an odd sort of reticence. "...and she was a senior officer of the Deuxième Bureau's cryptographical service."

"Crypto-whatacle? What does that mean?" I asked, completely in the dark about what cryptographical services do. Montclaire answered.

"She was a code-breaker, Fitz. Marie-Claire was a person expert in codes. Is that not so, Fleury?"

The Colonel frowned. "Rather more than that, Montclaire. Marie-Claire Bernard was France's top code-breaker and the Director of her unit within the DB, but even that is not the half of it." He and Picot exchanged glances. "She was also the genius creator of France's principal military communications code."

"Good Heavens!" I gasped. "A talented woman? I suppose so!"

"Indeed," said Fleury. "When we heard of her death there was a collective howl at the Bureau, I can assure you. Her loss to France is almost incalculable."

"But why didn't the Minister mention this to me, to start," Montclaire asked, with a hint of irritation in his voice. "And you, Picot?"

"Quite simply," said Picot, "the Minister of Justice does not know of Marie-Claire's secret life. The DB's internal operations are not something that is shared with many of those in the political world, because those are the very last people in the world you'd expect to keep any secret. Especially cabinet ministers." He paused. "And I have not told you 'til now because I needed Colonel Fleury's permission."

"Well, who did know then?" Montclaire asked, still annoyed.

"Except for those in the military intelligence bureaus, only the Prime Minister knows of Marie-Claire's role in the DB, we believe," Fleury said.

"But surely her fiancé, this Major Gargal, knew. After all, they were to be married," I suggested.

For some reason, both Fleury and Picot suddenly assumed the same look of surprise. Or, was it caution?

"There you have stumbled into the second issue that brings us here, Sir Francis. The fact is that Major Gargal is also an officer of the Deuxième Bureau."

Somehow, Montclaire did not seem nearly as surprised as I was by this latest revelation.

"She and Gargal were colleagues, then?" he asked.

"No. Not precisely," Fleury explained. "Gargal serves in a different element within the DB. His responsibilities do not touch upon codes and such."

"And what precisely does his unit do?" Montclaire followed.

"They track the activities of German agents who serve in friendly countries, under the diplomatic cover of Austria and Italy — Germany's allies."

"I see. Yes, of course," said Montclaire. Then there came a long pause, during which he rose, threw both hands in his pockets, and gazed out the library window into the rue de Longchamps in a vacant sort of way. When he turned again toward our guests it was to ask a more focused question.

"Let me be clear, Colonel. Was Gargal then aware of all that was happening in Marie-Claire's unit?"

"No. Not at all. The DB maintains a strict wall between units and information is only shared on a need-to-know basis, and only I may approve such sharing of information."

*How can we be sure of that?* I was thinking. *What two lovers share is not likely to be subject to approval by their boss.*

Fleury paused and clearly had said all he had come to convey about Marie-Claire's secret life. I was struck by how suddenly, and with no forewarning at all, our investigation of the murder of poor Marie-Claire Bernard had grown by another very interesting dimension. *What a tangled skein of crime we have here*, I mused, as the door closed behind our visitors.

When Picot and Fleury had gone, with assurances they would answer any further questions Montclaire might have, we settled into a day that was far more relaxed than I had expected. Montclaire remained inactive the next day as well, and so my curiosity led me to ask him why we were not out pursuing our investigation. "Surely there are lines to be followed and questions to answer," I urged.

"Oh yes, there certainly are plenty of both, Fitz, but I sense that it is time in our investigation to allow certain things to ripen. We allow the kneaded dough to rise before we bake the bread, eh."

Montclaire's intuition that something was about to happen proved uncanny. Picot appeared at our door the next morning, again brandishing a copy of the newspaper.

# Chapter Six
# Mademoiselle Claude Summons Us

"*Figaro* says Georges Joffre was last seen the morning of his disappearance at his bank, and one witness saw him enter a carriage in the company of two gentlemen. The hallmark of a kidnapping in broad daylight," said Picot. "Those two 'gentlemen' were thugs of the gambling syndicate, or I'll swim the Seine at midnight."

"No need to risk that, Picot. I don't think anyone would take your bet," said Montclaire. "Now we must keep watch for a body, perhaps floating in that same river you were willing to swim."

"What in the meantime?" I asked, thinking that Montclaire would wish to go after the gamblers, as the possible murderers of Marie-Claire also. It was Picot who spoke, adding to his report.

"Meanwhile, the three bowls are nowhere to be found. We have finished taking apart the apartment. No hiding places. No bowls. Did the gamblers take them? Or, perhaps Georges had them, and now the gamblers are pressuring him at knifepoint to hand them over."

"And, did the gamblers kill Marie-Claire in the first place to get them?" I added. "Twenty million francs is motive for murder, and then some."

"Good question," said Montclaire, rubbing his chin thoughtfully with his thumb and forefinger. "Perhaps the gamblers learned of the valuable bowls from Georges, tried to steal them from Marie-Claire, and something went wrong."

"Maybe the brave young woman put up a fight," I speculated.

"Exactly my theory of the thing, Sir France," said Picot, looking to Montclaire for agreement.

"But where are the bowls?" asked Montclaire. "If the gamblers got them from Marie-Claire, they would not need to kidnap Georges to get them. In that case, they would have taken him to silence him, and we may assume he is already dead. But, if the gamblers did not steal them, as you theorize, Picot, who did take them? Where are they? We cannot be confident of any theories at this point, no matter how nicely they fit what we know of the fact."

"This investigation seems to produce new questions constantly, without admitting any answers," I lamented.

Just then Petrovsky entered, more or less dragging a filthy street urchin by the collar of his ragged coat. The lad had a scrap of paper in his hand and a frightened look on his face. The giant Russian came to a full stop, with the boy dangling about ten inches above ground level, like a corpse hanging from a scaffold.

"What is it, Petrovsky?" Montclaire asked as the lad began to squirm and curse Petrovsky in a sort of gutter French that I only half understood. I could understand just enough to tell it was a soliloquy on the giant Russian's dubious parentage.

"This creature appeared at the door, Monsieur. He insists he must see you and none other."

Montclaire ordered the lad to stop squirming and cursing, and when he'd done so, he took the note from his hand and read it, as the boy continued to dangle from Petrovsky's hand. In a moment, Montclaire looked up with narrowed eyes and handed the scrap to Picot without comment. The detective read aloud.

*"The bowls are being sold by those who took them. It will cost you 5,000 FF to know where to find them. Bring the money tomorrow. Ask the boy."*

"Surely this is a sham," I scoffed. "Whoever sent that note will take your money and that will be the last of it. I mean to say — a note delivered by a street urchin. Someone has sent this boy to lead you into a trap."

"Hoy. Who you calling an 'urchin,' my man?" the lad protested, still in Petrovsky's clutches. "And what the hell's an 'urchin' anyway? I ain't no urchin, you English bastard."

Montclaire turned to the boy, who'd resumed his chorus of vulgar abuse, spitting and scoffing once again in a sort of obscure French.

"Boy, do you know the person who gave you this note?" Montclaire demanded.

"No," he replied with a sullen frown. Then hissed at me again.

"What did he tell you?"

"It weren't a 'he.' *She* told me I was to see that it went to Montclaire and none other."

"What sort of person was she?" Montclaire asked, giving me a side-long glance.

"She were a hag. That's what," he said nodding authoritatively. "And she give me a sou to bring you that paper."

"Where?" Montclaire persisted. "Where did this transaction take place?"

"An impasse, off the Rue de Lisbonne, near the Parc Monceau," he told, without hesitation. "Hoy, I'm an honest lad and you questions me like you was a *keuf*," he protested. I noticed that Picot started to give him a fist to the head, but then restrained himself. "Let me go!" he shouted at Petrovsky and once again began to squirm.

*Now there's a lad who knows what it means to be questioned by the gendarmes*, I was thinking to myself, when Montclaire scolded, "Release the boy, Petrovsky! Can't you see he's an 'honest lad'?"

Petrovsky dropped the foul-mouthed gutter-snipe, who began immediately to rearrange his clothing while renewing his barrage of curses, now flung mainly at the Russian. And once again my French was incapable of deciphering half of what he said. *Later,* I thought to myself, *I must ask Montclaire to school me in some of those words.*

"The note says I am to ask you something. What?" Montclaire asked.

"The hag told me to tell you where to go, eh."

"Where?"

"Do you know Montmartre?" the boy asked, doubtfully.

"Yes."

"There's a cabaret called Les Trois Canards, near the Cimetière de Montmartre? It's between the Rue des Abbesses and Rue Véron, eh?"

"Go on."

"The hag says you should go there tomorrow evening, around eleven o'clock. Ask for Mademoiselle Claude."

"And…?"

"That's all. That's what the old bitch told me to tell Montclaire. Are you sure you're Montclaire? You don't look like a *keuf*," the boy added, looking at Montclaire again, doubtfully.

Montclaire lapsed into silence for a moment, as I was thinking that the lad had told all he knew. But then I sensed he had heard something in the boy's slang that I had missed.

"Anything peculiar about the old hag," Montclaire asked. There you have it, I thought. It was the way the boy referred to the old woman.

The boy considered, giving each of us, in turn, a sly glance. Then his eyes narrowed. "Aye, there were. She ain't no Montmartre hag. She don't talk right. She talks proper French, like you, and don't appear to know street talk, eh?" the pint-sized thug explained with all the pride of one who was not fooled by a clever disguise.

"Thank you," said Montclaire, handing the boy a franc from his waistcoat pocket.

The boy's dirty face exploded with a smile as if he'd just been given a chateau in the Loir. Montclaire nodded and as Petrovsky escorted him to the door, he shouted his unwavering gratitude, once again delivered in slang that I could scarcely understand.

When the door had closed on the boy, Montclaire smiled. "That boy has the makings of a fine detective." I sniffed. Picot snorted, and then changed the subject.

"I suppose we know where to be tomorrow evening, around eleven o'clock."

I was pleased to hear that Picot and gendarmes would be in it with us. My first thought was that Montclaire was going to drag me into Montmartre in the middle of the night, dangling a bag stuffed with 5,000 FF for the amusement of every cutthroat lurking in one of Paris's seediest districts. It would have been just like him. In our long association, I reckoned that I had followed him into midnight ramblings through most of Paris's questionable neighborhoods, where I had been chased, shot at, knifed, and beaten by some of France's more accomplished criminals. Somehow, the notion of preparation gave me a new confidence that this time would be different.

Still, I was unconvinced by all the boy had said. "Pardon me, but all this continues to strike me as a sham. Someone is hoping to walk away with your 5,000 FF and that is all."

"That may well be," said Montclaire, "but consider. The disappearance of the bowls is not a well-known thing. It has been withheld from the newspapers and few knew they were in Marie-Claire's apartment. I believe we may have someone here who has information — perhaps only vague information — that will nonetheless be worth the price."

I remember harrumphing silently to myself.

"So, we wait until tomorrow then," Picot followed.

"No," said Montclaire. "We have an important mission today. We are going to see the one man in France who can tell us anything we wish to know about the missing bowls, except where to find them."

# Chapter Seven
# The Tears of Buddha

I learned only as we boarded Picot's coach that we were in for a drive that would take us across Paris to the Sorbonne, where Professor Raymond Baladeur was expecting us.

"Baladeur is France's foremost authority on Chinese art," Montclaire informed us, "and he is poised to answer any questions we have about the bowls. I sent him a note earlier this morning, telling him of our interest."

As we drove to the sweetly tingling sound of the little bells on our cab's horses, I mused about my notable deficiencies in French and so I decided to ask Montclaire about something the boy had said.

"What is a *keuf*?" I asked. The question seemed to explode like a bomb in the middle of a funeral. Picot's eyes bulged and his mouth fell open. Montclaire frowned.

"It is the foulest, most despicable word you can use to refer to a policeman, Colonel," Picot explained, in a huff.

"Oh."

Baladeur's office turned out to be a small nook in one corner of the University's court, crowded with bookcases stuffed with books, and all surfaces littered with stacks of papers. The Professor — a crumpled little man with long white hair and a scholarly stoop to his neck — greeted us with almost unbounded enthusiasm.

"Please, gentlemen. Please come in," he exclaimed, scurrying about the room to pull up chairs for us to sit. "Please, make yourselves comfortable."

As we gathered around a warm hearth in the corner of the study, Baladeur leaned forward, tossed a few coals on the grate, and then invited more of what Montclaire had already teased.

"You say, Monsieur, that you have news of three Tang bowls, of identical style and perfect design? From Wenshu and made during the reign of the Daizong Emperor?" he questioned almost in a whisper, his bird-like eyes bulging.

"Exactly," said Montclaire. "I am told by the art dealer, Dulac, that they are called *The Tears of Buddha*."

Baladeur gasped, covered his mouth with both hands, and then reeled back in his chair, such that I thought he would fall to the floor in a dead faint. As I rose to steady him, he managed to say, "Monsieur, you cannot know what you are saying. Do you have the least idea what you are telling one such as me?"

"Perhaps not," Montclaire answered, giving me and Picot a questioning look.

"It is as if you announced that I would find the riches of Solomon laid at my door tomorrow morning."

"How so, Professor?" I followed.

"Bien, Sir Frances. I will tell you. *The Tears of Buddha* are the rarest of all Chinese porcelain, from *any* dynasty! They are credited by those few who have seen them to be the very ideal — the perfection — of porcelain making. Someone such as me... well, I can only say that I have long hoped to see them before I die."

"I take it then that they have not been available for viewing in the recent past," said Montclaire.

"So far as I know they have *never* been on public or even private display, Monsieur. For the longest time, they were the most prized possession of the Chinese Emperors and were secreted away in the Forbidden City in Peking. Then, it is said that during the era of the Taiping Rebellion — about 1870, I understand — they were stolen, somehow, and have not been seen since. It was supposed by the art world that they were somehow taken by the Taiping and probably lost or destroyed. Those lunatics were capable of anything, you know."

"*Oui*," Montclaire agreed, "capable of anything."

Then, for some reason known only to him, the Professor launched into a tirade about what foul blisters the Taipings were, maundering on about their leaders and behavior for some time. Montclaire did not like to stop him, and so the passionate discourse continued as he stood and looked out the Professor's small window, collecting his thoughts I supposed. When Baladeur had worn himself to an emotional frazzle and was compelled to fall silent, Montclaire turned, with the one question he'd intended all along to ask the Professor.

"In all your experience, Professor, have you heard anything — the gossip of the art world, for example — about the bowls?"

Baladeur needed only a moment to consider the question. "Oh yes, Monsieur, but only one thing in all my years. When I was in Berlin several years ago — I suppose it was in 1899 — to attend a conference on Chinese porcelain at the Museum there, I heard the strangest rumor. Without foundation, it seemed, but whispered about."

Montclaire's eyes fixed and his jaw tightened. "And what was that, Professor?"

"I was told that the Kaiser, who is a keen collector, you know, was moving Heaven and Earth to obtain them. At any price."

"And…?"

"I have heard nothing since then and certainly nothing of how they might have come to France. That is simply too *fantastique* to contemplate."

"*Oui*," Montclaire agreed, with a quixotic smile. "Too *fantastique* indeed."

*Not so fantastique as that an old hag in Montmartre would have something to tell about anything that would fetch 5,000 FF,* I mused to myself. And then, for some reason, I shuddered.

# Chapter Eight
## Assassins

We met Picot next morning by prearrangement at a restaurant in the Boulevard Lannes, on the margins of the Bois de Boulogne. He greeted us with a face full of news.

"What is it, Picot?" Montclaire asked eagerly.

"Information. Overnight. From sources that have helped the Sûreté in the past very usefully. That is, we have a high level of confidence in what they report."

"And?" I pressed him.

"It seems Georges Joffre is alive and is being held by his gambling associates, to whom we already know he is deeply in debt."

"Yes?" Montclaire said.

"He is reportedly being held until his father pays his debts, and then some. A premium you might say. The gamblers are demanding payment by next week, or they'll kill young Joffre to make an example of him. Those same sources say Joffre's father has been told, but he has communicated nothing of this to us. They also say the old skinflint has balked at the price demanded and is attempting to negotiate with the kidnappers."

*Oh yes*, I thought to myself. *I'll wager old Joffre is desperate with concern for his son.*

"Anything about the Chinese bowls from your sources?" I asked.

"I was about to ask the same thing, Fitz," said Montclaire.

"No. Unfortunately, we've not been able to establish a connection between young Joffre's disappearance and the missing blows," Picot shrugged.

All this caused Montclaire to fall into one of his brooding silences. *No matter*, I thought. *I am famished and the clear morning air of the café has encouraged my appetite.* As Picot and I ordered breakfast, Montclaire gazed a nothing much. When he regained consciousness, he found that I had ordered his usual breakfast and it was in front of him. Picot resumed the conversation, this time with news that the Sûreté had found nothing in its vast files about someone named "Mademoiselle Claude".

"That is as much as I expected," Montclaire said. "It seems to be a name of convenience."

"But, who do you suppose this Mademoiselle Claude to be, then? If she is not an agent of the gamblers, what's her game?"

"A good question. Perhaps we'll find out once we have made her acquaintance this evening." Montclaire smiled.

"But you have not told me how you wish the Sûreté to act in this evening's meeting, Monsieur," Picot protested.

"That's quite simple, Picot. I do not wish you to act all. Whoever has designed this meeting wishes me to come alone. I don't suppose it will matter to them that Fitz comes with me, but if they detect surveillance by the Sûreté it will certainly disrupt things and we'll learn nothing. No, you should remain distant and allow Fritz and me to learn what we can.

My heart sank. Once again Montclaire was trusting in his ability to navigate any difficulty or danger and expecting me to share his confidence — and his fate.

The day grew colder with the evening shadows and so when it came time to depart rue de Longchamp, I was fitted out with my warmest jersey under my wool jacket and a wool cap. Montclaire dressed much the same. Between the two of us, we looked like a couple of credible French blokes of the working-class variety. Montclaire could do so from toe to tongue. I decided to keep my mouth shut and remain content to look the part.

We alighted from our cab some distance from the Cimetière. The cabbie accepted a franc to wait for us, but as he looked around in fright at the neighborhood, I had little confidence we'd find him there on our return.

We found the Boulevard de Clichy locked in a cold fog, which seemed to thicken as we made our way north toward the Rue Véron and the cabaret. Even at some distance from the place, we could hear the blast of glaring music. And at the door we were greeted by even louder music, coming from a small band of musicians playing traditional instruments and a crowd of patrons, singing in radical disharmony and dancing wildly to their rhythm.

"A *bal musette*," Montclaire observed. "Restrain yourself from joining the dance, *mon vieux*. We have other business," he smiled.

We found seats at a table to one side of the room, near where two fat men with large, soup strainer mustaches tended a long bar, singing enthusiastically to the music. They sang loudly and in radical disharmony as they served up cheap wine and other swill in mugs and tall glasses. Montclaire ordered two of the swill, and as we drank, I noticed patrons passing to and from a door at the back. When I asked Montclaire, who also seemed interested, he had only a brief reply.

"Opium."

"How will we find Mademoiselle Claude in all this?" I asked, in a whisper.

"At first, we'll hope she finds us. If not, we'll be forced to search for her, eh."

The swill was disgusting, but we downed it like it was the divine elixir of life. When a drunken woman finally approached us, I was sure it was Mademoiselle, but she was only a whore offering her services out back. Happily, Montclaire told her something that sent her away with a smile. When the waiter returned, Montclaire asked about Mademoiselle, a question that did not seem to surprise at all. The waiter left without an answer, but soon returned and pointed with a nod of his head to the door at the back, where patrons were still coming and going.

Montclaire rose immediately and moved toward the door. I followed. At the door, we met a young woman — dazed and wobbly — coming out. Inside, we descended stone steps to a lower level, where a long stone passage led twenty feet to another door. At that door, a rough sort of character with a broad smile and a mouth full of rotten teeth stopped us.

"Don't stop when you go in," he ordered. "Go right to the far wall where you'll find a door."

We did as we were told. Inside, we moved past rough-made cots, stacked one on top of another, that lined each wall, where opium fiends smoked their black gum from clay pipes and where some who'd already imbibed were passed out and even hanging off their cots. The place gave off a sickening musty scent as if a cheese had died there, in painful circumstances. I put my scarf to my nose and followed Montclaire. When we reached the door at the end, Montclaire knocked. A man with a raspy voice opened it a crack and demanded, "What'd ye want?"

"Mademoiselle Claude," said Montclaire.

The door closed and then opened. A small man with a bald head and eyes like a frog greeted us with a nod and a suspicious look, and then urged us on, down yet another dingy passage, toward a single door at the end. "Knock when ye get there. She don't like it if ye don't," he warned.

Our knock at the ominous door brought an immediate command. "*Entrée!*"

When we opened the door and peered in, my eyes must have bulged to see what lay inside. The room, richly lined in tapestries and bookcases, holding volumes bound in rich vellum, appeared to be a library of sorts, and in the middle, behind a large ornate desk of mahogany there sat the smallest woman I'd ever seen. The foul-mouthed street urchin had chosen not to tell us the most striking thing about the old hag. A dwarf, and then some, she wore a large blonde wig and stank of cheap perfume.

Shadows partly concealed her features, because the entire room was lighted only by a low lamp on the desk.

"Welcome," said the dwarf, in a deep, resonant voice.

"Mademoiselle Claude?" Montclaire asked.

"Yes. That is me, and you are Montclaire? I have heard much of you and longed to meet you, Monsieur. And I must say, you are even more handsome than I have heard."

When Montclaire had introduced me, the little woman invited, "Sit. Both of you. Please."

Montclaire took the invitation as a signal to state his interest.

"We're here at your beckoning, Mademoiselle. For what purpose? I understand that you have information about some objects that we seek."

"Ah, yes, the bowls," she said gleefully. "Yes, quite so. I have information that is... well, it is a commodity that is for sale, Montclaire. Have you the 5,000 FF? That is the price for my information, pure and simple."

Montclaire drew a thick envelope from his inside pocket but retained it in his hand. Mademoiselle Claude's eyes widened to see it, and then she leaned back in her chair and started cackling. She went on cackling for some time, such that I started looking at the ceiling.

"Well then, it only remains for me to earn your price, eh?" She paused, obviously collecting her thoughts, and as she did so, Montclaire cast an eye about the room. I did the same, thinking it would be useful to know if there was another way out. There wasn't.

"I fear I cannot tell you all you wish to know, but I can tell you some things of value. If you consider those things worth the price, I will accept that fat envelope in your hand." She resumed her inane cackling, but this time cut it short.

"Information is a thing of great variations in value," said Montclaire, looking at the envelope.

"Allow me then to tell you only what I know for certain and you may judge of its value."

"Fair enough."

"First, I can assure you that the gamblers who have taken young Joffre have nothing whatever to do with the bowls you seek, but perhaps you already knew that. I thought so, at first, but I've been able to establish the truth of what I say. What I can add is that there are murmurings in dark quarters — places where my informants reside — that the bowls are indeed for sale. Yes. Someone has them and is trying to sell them, but so far that person has not made a deal. I understand the reason for this is that this person is frightened of making a mistake and so must be careful to find just the right buyer."

Montclaire raised an eyebrow. Mademoiselle appeared to take this as a gesture of approval and smiled to indicate her satisfaction.

"One other thing, Montclaire. And this may be the most valuable information I have to sell."

"Oh?"

"From other sources, I learn there is indeed a buyer seeking the bowls and that a sale is in the offing."

"And?" Montclaire encouraged, leaning forward in his chair.

"The buyer is said to be…."

The little old hag stopped herself in mid-sentence and smiled, obviously to create valuable suspense, all the while staring at the envelope.

"…is said to be German. A German whose purse is bottomless, they say."

Montclaire considered for a moment, then dropped the envelope on the desk.

"Fair enough, Mademoiselle. You have earned your price. However…."

A small hand reached out and took up the fat envelope.

"However," Mademoiselle smiled, as she thumbed through the notes in the envelope.

"…I'll hope to hear anything in addition that you learn about the bowls, eh?"

"Of course, Monsieur. Your money is good." And with that Mademoiselle Claude tucked the envelope in the drawer of her desk and folded her hands, signaling that the interview had reached its end.

As Montclaire and I retraced our way through the passage, the opium den, the cabaret, and then into the alley, I could not help but scold. "Really, Montclaire. Trusting the word of a Montmartre hag who operates her business out of an opium den? Have you taken leave of your senses?"

He smiled in his sardonic way at my characterization and question. "Sometimes, *mon vieux*, the truth comes in strange packages and is to be found in odd places."

No sooner had Montclaire made his *bon mot* than I heard something that sounded like a bee zing past my head. I knew from experience that the buzz was not a bee, but before I could fall to the ground, we both heard the report of a pistol shot. Montclaire had pulled me down and behind a dustbin that stood to one side of the impasse.

"What the…," I uttered, but then heard the sound of running, down the impasse toward the Rue Véron. Montclaire reacted quickly, stood, pulled a revolver from his coat, and discharged six quick ones down the impasse, apparently without effect. No wonder. The fog was so thick he could not have seen a target.

Then we heard the unexpected. A loud groan from the alley. Chancing it, we ran to the noise, in time to find a body lying to one side, against a wall. The wounded man was gurgling, spitting blood, and groaning incoherently. And then we heard it. The dying man said only one word before he fell silent. "Gottverdammt."

We looked at each other in amazement. "Great Scott, Montclaire! The blighter's a German!"

For a moment, he lay so still that I knew he had died. Then, he opened wide his eyes, and seeing us standing over him, he began to plead for help, this time in French. I didn't like to disappoint him in his Gawdawful condition, but he was begging help from Gérard de Montclaire — probably the least forgiving man in France. Unforgiving especially toward someone who'd just tried to shoot him.

Assistance would do no good anyway, I quickly concluded. He was a pitiful sight, and just as my heart was going out to him, in lieu of help, Montclaire kicked him a good one in the head. It was then the chap did the next best thing. He died. *Not very sporting of Montclaire*, I thought, *but the feller was an assassin after all.*


Montclaire said nothing, but quickly fell to a knee beside the corpse and began to rifle through the man's pockets and to check the labels in his clothing.

"Nothing," he groused, picking up the man's pistol and examining it as well.

When he stood, still holding the pistol, he said, "There's nothing about this fellow to suggest he is German. Even his pistol is French."

"What does that mean?" I asked.

"I cannot be sure, but there is one thing it suggests."

Before I could ask what, Montclaire had taken me by the forearm and was dragging me down the impasse toward the Rue Véron.

"Quick, Fitz. We must get out of here. That fellow might have a mate, who is looking for him, and us, even now. I can't count on another lucky miss in a fog like this."

In only a few minutes we'd passed the Rue Véron and had come upon the Boulevard Clichy, right near where our cab was waiting. We boarded. Montclaire ordered the driver, "6 Rue de Longchamp, my friend, and quick!"

As the cab coursed toward the Cimetière, Montclaire surprised me by asking a question that I thought had an obvious answer.

"That thug was waiting for us to emerge from the cabaret. It was an arranged attempt on our lives. Who do you suppose hired it?"

"That foul blister, Mademoiselle Claude, of course. She was the only person who knew we would emerge from the cabaret, eh?"

"We cannot know who Mademoiselle Claude might have told about our meeting, but it seems to me that we have excited the fears of someone."

"Perhaps that someone is the person most interested in obtaining those bowls."

"Yes, and that someone seems to be a German."

"Maybe *the* German."

Montclaire raised an eyebrow at my suggestion.

# Chapter Nine
## The Code Breakers

For a while, we continued our drive in silence. Then I decided to ask, "Back there, Montclaire. In the alley. You said it meant something the dead man's clothing had no labels, his pockets were empty, and his pistol was French. What did you mean?"

"Those are all the marks of the professional, Fitz. A trained assassin."

"Oh?"

"In his agony, he made the mistake of saying something in German. Otherwise, we would not have known his origins."

"Yes, I suppose so."

"I'll only say further that someone like Mademoiselle Claude would have hired a local thug to do her killing — not someone of our man's quality."

As was so often his way, Montclaire then retreated into a thoughtful silence and into some land of the mind where he was unreachable. He brooded the remainder of our journey home and then went directly to his bed-chamber, without so much as a *dormez bien*.

No matter. Wishing me a good sleep could not have forestalled what was in store. A largely sleepless night, during which my weary brain leaped from one thing to another, like a breathless stag over hedges, trying to figure out what connection there could be between Mademoiselle Claude, Germans, and Chinese bowls. Once I woke up, I could swear that someone had said, "*Gottverdammt!*" Then, I lay awake, considering. *Is the Kaiser so eager to have those bowls — his avarice so great — that he would sanction the murder of a young woman, and then Montclaire and me? And why did Montclaire seem to discount so easily the idea that Mademoiselle Claude had arranged for our murders?* As I turned relentlessly from one side to another and from one quandary to another, what was supposed to be a good sleep became a continuous horizontal headache.

Montclaire shared none of his suspicions with me the next morning, as I toyed with the buttered roll in the middle of my plate and dreaded the next sip of café noir. Somehow, my headache was refusing to subside, now that I had brought myself to vertical, and so I waited patiently for Petrovsky to mix a preparation for my head. While I waited, I moaned, not least because I was forced to endure my headache while looking at the disturbing pictures that festooned Montclaire's breakfast room walls — pictures he'd bought a year earlier at an exhibition from an oily little Spaniard squirt named Pablo something-or-other. Collectively they were enough to make any headache critical.

Finally, Petrovsky arrived with the very same remedy I'd often recommended myself to chaps who had been out on a riotous evening. A raw egg stirred into a glass of Worcestershire Sauce, with a bit of pepper powder mixed in — to give it that certain something that says, "Cheer up! It could be worse!"

Just as I downed the dreadful mixture, Montclaire announced his plan for the morning.

"It is time to visit the Deuxième Bureau, Fitz. Marie-Claire was a valued officer there and so we must take greater account of that part of our puzzle. It is also where we will find her grieving fiancé, who may have something to tell about her last days."

*Marie-Claire's employment was certainly an odd thing, but why was it part of our concern, I wondered? Besides, it was clear from our first interview with Fleury that the DB didn't much like our prying around in the subject of codes.*

Still, whatever Montclaire found interesting — however vague — seemed a legitimate thing to me. I had learned by long experience to trust his instincts. So as we passed the Trocadéro and made for the Seine Bridge, I decided to put my doubts aside for the moment and to think about what Montclaire might hope to learn from the DB. I had not concluded much before we turned into the precincts of Les Invalides, where DB Headquarters was located at that time.

Fleury was expecting us, and as we entered his office I noticed he had with him a young officer, who I assumed to be his deputy. When the introductions were made, I learned that the young officer — a tall, handsome man with open countenance — was François Gargal, Marie-Claire's fiancé.

Montclaire turned directly to the reason for our visit.

"I am particularly pleased to speak with you, Major, but first please accept our sincere condolences on your loss. I can only imagine how difficult it is for you to carry on at a time like this, and we all appreciate your courage. I regret the need to ask you some questions, but you will understand that we wish to get to the bottom of Marie-Claire's death."

The young man merely nodded and then, looking down, said almost in a whisper, "Thank you, Monsieur. I quite understand."

"In the past days and weeks had you noticed anything amiss in Marie-Clair's mood or behavior? Anything at all? No matter how slight?"

Gargal answered quickly. "No, not at all. Marie-Claire was her usual charming and happy self until the last moment I saw her."

"And when was that?"

"Here. The day before... the day before she died."

"And all was well between the two of you?"

The question seemed to surprise the Major, but once again he responded quickly. "Very well. In fact, never better. We looked forward to our wedding, which was to be next month."

The Major dropped his head in obvious pain as he said that last. Montclaire paused to allow time for him to recompose.

"I know this is painful for you, Major, but it's necessary if we are to find the culprits, you understand."

"Oh yes," Gargal replied, eagerly. "I understand and I want to help as I am able."

"*Bon*. Did Marie-Claire mention to you that she had some valuable Chinese porcelain bowls in her possession? Bowls that she was attempting to sell on behalf of her family?"

"I knew the family wished to sell some bowls, but I did not know Marie-Claire had them. No. I thought that Pierre — that's her father — was selling them."

He gasped.

"Good God! Did Marie-Claire have them? Do you think that's why...?"

Montclaire did not answer but instead shifted to another line of questioning that I had anticipated.

"Did Marie-Claire keep a diary — a journal, perhaps? Young ladies often keep such things, you know."

Gargal seemed surprised by the question.

"Well then, I am not sure. I do not think she ever mentioned it to me if she did. But I cannot be certain."

Montclaire paused and offered the two a cigarette from his case. Neither accepted, but Montclaire took one, lit it, and drew on it for a moment. As the smoke wafted across Fleury's office, it seemed to me that Montclaire must have exhausted his questions for the two. However, that was not so. Turning to Fleury, he asked, "Marie-Claire's work for the DB, Colonel? I know that she directed the Code Section. I wish to ask you more particularly about some elements of her work."

Fleury and Gargal exchanged glances and then Gargal rose. "If you gentlemen will excuse me, I have duties that require my presence elsewhere."

"Of course," said Montclaire, standing and shaking the Major's hand. "You have been most helpful, Major. Most helpful."

When Gargal had gone, Fleury looked at me in a way that at first took me off guard but then I realized the issue.

"Have no concern about Colonel FitzMaurice as I advised the other day," said Montclaire. "What you tell him is as safe as what you tell me. I vouch for him as I would my own brother."

Fleury seemed to accept Montclaire's vouchsafe. Now lowering his voice to a confidential whisper, he said, "I was less than candid with you the other day when I told you of Marie-Claire's work."

"Oh?"

"Yes. Well, Marie-Claire Bernard was not just one of our code makers, though that would have been significant enough."

Montclaire leaned in.

"Marie-Claire and her unit had just made a breakthrough that gave us complete access to the German diplomatic code."

Montclaire's eyes opened wide. "How many people, in the DB or Government, knew of this breakthrough?"

"Very few, as you can imagine. It was closely held. Within the DB, only myself and, of course, Marie-Claire herself. In the Government, only the Minister of Army, the Prime Minister, and, of course, the Minister of Foreign Affairs."

"Have we noticed anything in the behavior of the Germans that would indicate they are aware of this breakthrough and are reacting to it?"

"No. Not as yet," Fleury said, a worried look on his face. "But Marie-Claire's murder has us on high alert for such indications, I can assure you. And as you can imagine it is a priority with us to notice anything that would indicate the Germans are on to us. That is the job of Major Gargal's unit."

Montclaire leaned back in his chair.

"But there's more. Oh yes, much more." Fleury continued, his whole face excited.

Montclaire gave me a sidelong glance.

"Breaking the German diplomatic code was one thing, but for some reason, Marie-Claire had not had much success against another code the Germans use — the one by which the German Intelligence — our counterparts in the Geheime Nachreichtendienst der Heeres — communicate with their agents in far-flung embassies. She found it to be a much trickier code," he added, narrowing his eyes.

"But there was progress on that as well?"

"That is why I asked you here today. I had to gain permission from the Prime Minister to convey it to you."

Montclaire's face did not conceal his annoyance.

"Fleury, I am tiring of your habit of telling me the pertinent facts of Marie-Claire's work in dribs and drabs. Why this delay? Why did you require the additional permission of the Prime Minister? Why were you not candid with me from the beginning? You treat me as if I am suspect... not competent to receive secret information!"

By the end of his questioning, Montclaire sounded angry. Fleury looked down with all the shame of a schoolboy taking a scolding for an incomplete lesson book.

"I regret it, Montclaire, but... er... there has been a continuing difficulty in all this and...."

"What difficulty is that?" Montclaire cut him short.

"To be quite frank...."

"Yes. Do," Montclaire said tersely.

"To be quite frank," he resumed, expelling a deep breath, "It is Sir Francis. His presence in all this has created sensitivities. Sir Francis, you see, is *not* French."

He said that last raising his chin, defiantly.

"He is a serving officer in His Majesty's army. There are secrets that the French Government has not seen fit to share with the British, despite the closeness of our present relations. So, you can see that...."

"Yes, I can see quite clearly, Fleury. You needn't continue your explanation. And I take it that you have now obtained all the permissions necessary to tell me all I need to know?"

"Indeed," he said, swallowing hard. There followed an uneasy silence, during which I inspected every square inch of the ceiling.

"In that case, Fleury, I suggest you take the trouble to inform our British friends, as you are about to inform Sir Francis and me."

"We have already done so, Montclaire."

"Good. Now that all this bother about who is French and who is not French is settled, you were preparing to convey something to me? What? Convey what?"

"Just this. Marie-Claire was certain she was on the brink of breaking that code as well. She reported to me just a few days before her death that she had figured out some important characteristics of that code, and she was confident that in a short time she would be able to break it also."

For a moment, I rocked back a little at what Fleury was saying, because the ability to intercept and to read an adversary's most secret communications, I knew, was an enormous advantage. It took me only a moment to wonder if the French had seen fit to share this new information with Whitehall or even the Prime Minister, but then I realized that Fleury's reluctance to allow me to hear all this probably meant that they had not. Montclaire decided to ask.

"And you say this secret — this information about an impending breakthrough — was not shared with any foreign capitals? Not even the British."

Fleury looked at his hands for a brief moment but avoided glancing at me. "No, not even the British. Not until now."

When we re-boarded our cab in the court of Les Invalides, I asked Montclaire the one question that interested me most.

"Now that we have learned of Marie-Claire's pending breakthrough, Montclaire, does that change how we must think of this investigation? I mean to say, are we looking for a Chinese porcelain thief or not? Or, are we now obliged to include that code business?"

"That 'code business,' as you call it, has always been in the frame of our investigation, *mon vieux*. Ever since we learned of Marie-Claire's profession. Now, however, we must move it a little forward in our view. It takes on greater importance, if only because we now learned what she was on the brink of achieving. The question must now be, 'If the Germans knew Marie-Claire was moving through their cherished codes like a dose of salts, would they decide to kill her?'

"There's another question even more troubling."

"Oh?"

"Yes. If they knew how close she was to breaking their cherished code, how did they know that?"

"A good question too, of course," but still I insisted, "It seems to me that important as all that code business was, Marie-Claire was almost certainly killed by whoever wanted those bowls. Consider. She had them in her possession up to the moment she was killed, and when she was murdered, they disappeared. What more proof is required?"

Montclaire did not refute my assertion even if he had cared to do so. As was so often the case with him, he merely shrugged and then retreated into his own thoughts. Soon, there entered an unexpected actor in the case, whose evidence tended to complicate things even further. I was taken aback by what she told us, because it did not support my theory of things at all.

# Chapter Ten
# Elsie Boudreau

Montclaire remained what I can only call inert for several days, show-ing almost no interest in the investigation. Notably a man of action, he could at times adopt an oyster-like reserve. Most days, he retreated to his study and there resumed his one enthusiasm outside of crime — the study of the remotest origins of the French language. I began to suspect that he was at a complete impasse and had no choice but to wait for something to happen — something that would provide a springboard for action. That came quickly, in the visit of a beautiful young woman was that springboard, who served to draw Montclaire once more away from his linguistic researches and to the matter of Marie-Claire's awful murder.

It was a rainy morning in Paris — the sort of day you suppose no callers would come. And yet, just after breakfast, Petrovsky entered the library to announce a visitor.

"A young woman wishes to see you, Monsieur," he said with a doubtful look. "She says she is a relation of Madame Bernard."

Montclaire's eyebrows raised a little, as he gave me a questioning glance.

"By all means, Petrovsky. Show the young lady in."

In almost the next instant there appeared at our door an extraor-dinarily handsome woman, tall and willowy with long black hair, finely made features, and a dress that emphasized her exceptional figure. She smiled faintly, as she extended her hand, first to Montclaire and then to me.

"I am Elsie Boudreau, Monsieur. Marie-Claire Bernard was not only my cousin but also my good friend," she said, with a tearful voice. "I have learned from my uncle — Marie-Claire's father — that you are investigating her…."

She paused to gather her courage to say the word.

"--- her murder. Of course, I wish to do all I can to help and so I've come to tell you one thing that might assist you."

"And what is that one thing, Mademoiselle?" Montclaire asked, at the same time gesturing to offer her a seat.

"I am not sure I can be precise," she said, taking a chair, "but it seemed to me that something was troubling Marie-Claire in the week or so before her death. She did not say so at first, but I could tell by her demeanor. She was usually so happy and outgoing, but of late she was troubled by something."

"And?" Montclaire encouraged.

"And so, I finally asked her what it was that so obviously troubled her. At first, she did not wish to confide it to me, but then she decided to unburden. Even then, however, she was not specific."

"How do you mean?"

"She would only say that she was troubled by 'a friend.' That something had strained her relations with a good friend. Well, that's just the sort of thing that would dampen the spirits, and so I was sympathetic, but I did not press Marie-Claire to tell me more. I assumed things would resolve themselves in the long run and so I did not think much more of it. Until that is... until Marie-Claire was killed. Since then, I have wondered if her trouble with a friend might in some way have had something to do with her... with her murder."

"You say she said no more at all about this 'good friend'. No indication at all of who it might be. Nothing?"

"No, nothing. She did not wish to tell me, and so I did not press her."

Montclaire rested his chin on his fist and reflected. Then he asked, "As Marie-Claire's good friend yourself, do you have any speculation who she was troubled by?"

"I have wondered about that myself, Monsieur, but I do not have a notion. Marie-Claire had many good friends and so it could have been any one of several persons."

"Did Marie-Claire ever speak to you of some valuable Chinese porcelain bowls? Bowls that might have had any part in her concern with her good friend?"

"She did tell me several weeks ago that she was representing her family in the sale of some items, but no more than that. She was not specific."

"On another matter, Mademoiselle, if you please. Do you know if your cousin kept a diary?"

"I'm not sure, but I believe she did. Once she mentioned as much to me."

Montclaire smiled, and then paused again to consider. I expected another question of our beautiful visitor, but he had none. Mlle. Boudreau rose to depart. As Montclaire took her elbow to escort her to the door, I wondered if she might be holding back something. Just short of the door, she turned suddenly, as if remembering.

"Oh yes. There is one other thing, Monsieur. Something I had almost forgotten until you asked me to speculate."

"What is that, Mademoiselle? We are eager to hear it."

"It was only a day or two later — after she had spoken of her friend — that she said something I found peculiar. She said... well, I cannot remember her words exactly, but she said that trust between even the best of friends is a frail thing. Yes, that is about what she said. I found it an odd thing to say, just out of the blue. But I remember thinking that it might have had something to do with her strained relations with her friend."

"That is a very useful thing to know, Mademoiselle. Thank you for your trouble in coming to see me. You've been very helpful to my investigation."

That assurance caused the young woman to show a faint smile, for the first time since her arrival. She turned and as she walked through the door Montclaire followed her with an intense eye.


When she had gone, Montclaire lingered at the door for a moment, considering what Elsie Boudreau had told us, or perhaps still just a little taken with the young woman's considerable charms.

"What do you make of this 'friend' business?" I asked. "Not very specific if you ask me. How are we to learn anything more definite that would be of help? And is it even useful information at all? Friends have disputes all the time. We might waste our time making too much of such a thing."

"It's quite simple, Fitz. We cannot know at the moment, but Elsie Boudreau — for some reason — attached great importance to Marie-Claire's troubled spirit and so she is telling us, in effect, to investigate it. And so, we will. We will tuck that fact neatly into our thickening dossier of things that matter in this case, eh. It's a matter of trusting what amounts to Elsie intuition, you see."

That did not seem to me to be much on which to base an effort and I said as much. No sooner had I pronounced than he narrowed his eyes and crinkled his nose at me and then raised his chin to look down the misshapen thing.

"Why do you cast a crinkled nose at me, Montclaire?" I huffed.

"Because you are being far too English, *mon ami*. Let your Gallic self take command." And then he smiled.

# Chapter Eleven
# Madame Soyeuse and the Professor

*My 'Gallic self' indeed!* What he meant by that apparent barb at the English left me in a bit of a snit all afternoon. I decided that it was probably best to observe what Montclaire would eventually decide to make of Mlle. Bourdeau's evidence and to base my notions of the case on the solid evidence I had obtained from reading the many *romans policiers* which were then becoming all the rage, and particularly those of that American chap, E.A. Allen. I knew from these that the detective must be dogged and unswerving in pursuing the solid evidence before him, and in this case that was clearly the theft of the dashed bowls. *We must be dogged in pursuing the thief,* I thought to myself, *because in doing that we will surely find the murderer.* Then I said so to Montclaire, based on my reading of the detective novels.

He tossed me a quick look of sympathy and then pronounced on my reading as he had never before done.

"Fitz, you continually site this *outré* literature of yours and particularly that American person. That fellow is an *author*, Fitz — a writer — and you know very well what authors are."

"No. What?" I said with a defiant toss of my head.

"They are mainly louts and ne'er-do-wells... loungabouts and opium-eaters who cannot make their livelihood in any legitimate occupation, and so they pander nonsense to the public at a half-sou per word. Those people are not to be trusted in their judgment, *mon ami. Pas du tout!*"

I decided not to contest the point because Montclaire had formed a prejudiced opinion and was not to be talked out of it. Just to show how wide of the mark he could sometimes be, I was shocked when later that evening he informed me that he had arranged for us to meet a person who I knew to be one of the least reputable people in Paris, but whom he portrayed as the one person who might be able to put us onto the bowls.

"It will interest you to know that I have contacted Madame Soyeuse," he said with a playful lilt in his voice.

"Oh, and what has he to do with this business?"

"I am not sure that Madame will be able to provide any direct evidence, but I am hoping to use his vast resources in the underworld to put us in contact with those who are likely to know at least part of what we want to know."

"And what is that?"

"Who has the bowls and where are they? I have asked Madame to strain every resource, no matter the cost, to put us onto answers to some questions I have."

"And has he? So we are expecting a visit from Madame Soyeuse, eh?"

"Not quite. Madame does not wish to be seen entering my apartment or even in public conversation with me. Madame asserts that would be a very dangerous thing just now and so he proposed we meet discreetly."

"Where?"

"In the Parc de La Muette, at eleven o'clock. Madame has given me directions to the location where our coaches will meet and where we may speak in private."

"Am I invited to this assignation?"

"Of course. Madame asked especially if you will attend. You know that Madame has a special fondness for you, Fitz." He smiled.


The small park called La Muette is an extension of the Bois de Boulogne, where there is located an old chateau. It lay nearby and just north of our apartment and so it took only a few minutes to reach the location in the park where Madame Soyeuse wished to meet. Our coach drew-up to a low wall and steps that were illuminated by a single gaslight, in a secluded part of La Muette. I knew by reputation that the park was not to be trusted at night, and so as we alighted, I felt reassuringly for the Webly in my coat pocket. The recent attempt on Montclaire's life added to my sense of danger.

We waited, stretching our legs and smoking, as the night's chill brought a rolling fog into the park. That and the glow of the gaslight's illumination in the haze gave the chateau a sinister aspect. Soon, a coach drew up and from it stepped Madame Soyeuse, owner of La Terminal — the most successful brothel in Paris. As usual, he was turned out in the very most elegant of *haute couture* and, as he spied Montclaire, he smiled broadly. Offering a hand as he approached, Montclaire took it and bowed in the most gentlemanly fashion, while I acknowledged Madame with a proper tip of the bowler.

"Dear, dear Montclaire," he gushed. "It has been far too long since I've seen you, and I am bound to say that you are as handsome as I remember.

"And Colonel," he said turning to me. "What a pleasure to see you again, also, my dear."

"May I say we are delighted to see you, Madame?" said Montclaire, "and I notice that you are as radiant as ever, even in the dim light of that lamp."

Madame smiled, and though I could not make it out, I am sure he blushed just a little.

With all of the *pourparlers* safely out of the way, Montclaire got down to the business at hand. I pulled the collar of my greatcoat around my ears, as comfort against the night's advancing chill.

"It's getting on to be a chilly evening, Madame, and so I won't detain you with further niceties."

Madame nodded and then shivered slightly. His evening gown and light cloak were insufficient protection against the cold.

"As you may know, I am presently investigating the murder of Marie-Claire Bernard."

"Ah, old Joffre's daughter," he said, in a knowing way.

"*Oui*, and I am particularly eager at the moment to know the whereabouts of some rare artifacts that were known to be in the young woman's possession but which are now missing."

"Oh yes. *The Tears of Buddha.*"

Montclaire's eyes widened a bit and one eyebrow rose.

"You are surprised, dear boy, that I am aware of such a thing? *Sacré*, you do underestimate me sometimes. You know very well it is my business to know such things. That is why we're here, *n'est pas?*"

"Exactly," said Montclaire. "Exactly. Is there anything you can tell that will help me find those bowls? Anything at all."

"Unfortunately, I am unable, myself."

Montclaire's face dropped a bit.

"But, I can put you onto someone who will be able to tell you all that is known, if anyone can. I will arrange it for you, at great cost to myself."

"Oh?"

"But first I want your assurance that you'll not share the name I am about to give you with the Sûreté and that you'll forget it yourself as soon as you have made your inquiry."

Montclaire pursed his lips and frowned. "Not possible, Madame. Etienne Picot is in this thing with me and I cannot exclude him."

Madame started to turn to walk away but then checked himself. "Very well, but Picot must agree to hold it in strictest confidence, within the Sûreté."

"Agreed!" Montclaire said, eagerly.

Madame took from his sachet a scrap of paper and the stub of a pencil and quickly scribbled a name. Handing the scrap to Montclaire, he drew it back quickly. "You'll not fail me on this, Montclaire? I am counting on you."

Montclaire nodded and then took the scrap, read it, and handed it back to Madame Soyeuse.

"Thank you, Madame. Thank you very much indeed."

Not bothering to linger in the cold night, Madame turned toward his coach. As he opened the door, however, he turned and, looking earnestly at Montclaire, said again, "You'll not fail me on this, Montclaire."

Montclaire nodded.

As Madame's coach took to the drive that led south out of La Muette, Montclaire turned to me and smiled. "That is the last name I expected to see, Fitz, but it's a name that gives me hope we'll have an answer."

When we were snugly in our coach and coursing smartly toward the rue de Longchamp, I asked. "What name was that? That yields such confidence."

"Lucien Radine," he answered. "Professor Lucien Radine."

"Not another Professor! This business seems full of them. Sorry, old man, but the name means nothing to me. Who is *this* Professor?"

"*Oui.* Another professor, but one with a difference. Radine no longer has a university position, because he is a criminal."

"What!"

"He was a noted authority upon Asian antiquities, to rival Professor Baladeur, until he was convicted of attempting to steal a national treasure of France!"

"If that is so, why have I never heard of him?"

Montclaire looked at me with that rare quandary in his face about whether or not he should tell me something.

"Because, *mon vieux*, Radine's crime was so troubling and so offensive to French pride that it was kept from the public gaze. The few journalists who learned anything of it were pressured into silence, and Radine's trial was strictly *in-camera*. Radine was tried under laws that treated him as if he were a national traitor, which he certainly was."

"Good Heavens then! What was his crime?"

Montclaire looked at me again with reservations but then decided to proceed.

"He plotted with a gang of Italians — based in Milan — to steal France's greatest treasure."

"What?"

"The Mona Lisa!"

When Montclaire uttered those last two words, I reeled just a little in my seat. "The Mona Lisa! But how? How could one possibly take such a thing? From the Louvre?"

"It was an audacious plot, Fitz. Radine and his cronies had bribed several of the guards at the Museum and were in the very act of removing the painting when a passing gendarme — a new recruit, in fact — happened to notice their van outside the commercial loading dock at the Louvre. He thought it odd that a delivery would be made at that time of night, and so he waited and observed. When the thieves emerged with a crate, rather than to deliver one, he blew his whistle and summoned help. Radine and his cronies were caught in the act, right there on the loading dock. Radine was sentenced to forty years. That was seven years ago, and the Professor spent five years in *La prison de la Santé* since then, in solitary confinement."

"I say it again. Good Heavens! What a crime! And to think that virtually no one has heard of it. I am sure that young gendarme must have been rewarded."

"You have that one right, *mon ami*. That young gendarme was Etienne Picot."

I was stunned yet again by the realization of young Picot's achievement, but when I recovered it was to ask, "But, where shall we find this Professor now? Fled the country, I suppose."

"No. You might think he would retreat to live with his co-conspirators in Milan, but he still resides in France. My last information about him said that he was released from prison and is living quietly in Deauville, where he enjoys a certain reputation for success with the rich English women who visit. We will find out if Picot can confirm that, and if I am correct, we must visit the good Professor, eh?"


Picot was indeed able to confirm by next evening and so the following morning we found ourselves, Picot included, on the train from the Gare Saint-Lazare, bound for Deauville. As we passed swiftly out of the environs of Paris and moved through the beautiful Forest of Saint-Germain-en-Laye, I gazed constantly out the window of our carriage, turning over and over in my mind that the man we sought would provide the key to the mystery of what had happened to the three bowls and who had murdered Marie-Claire Bernard to get them. Occasionally, I glanced over at my companions, both happily immersed in reading pages of a dossier on Radine that Picot had brought from the Sûreté's file and oblivious to the beauties of the Seine, as our train skirted it for miles along our way to the northwest.

"One thing puzzles me a little, Picot, and I find no answer in this dossier," Montclaire finally said.

"What is that, Monsieur?"

"How did Radine manage to earn his release from prison so soon, after attempting to do what he did? Sentenced to forty years, he served only five?"

"Ah," Picot leaned back, "there you have me. I can only tell what has been whispered since that time."

"What then?"

"That he was able to bargain for his freedom by... and here is where my information is sketchy... by giving information of great value to France, on a matter of grave national importance."

"What information was that?" I followed.

Picot frowned. "I do not know. But, it must have been something of supreme importance," he concluded, shaking his head.


Closer to Deauville, my thoughts turned to what sort of chap Radine would be. An elderly professor, now attending entirely to some researches on the history of art, or, as Montclaire speculated, one involved in other affairs altogether?

We arrived at the bustling Gare de Trouville-Deauville in mid-afternoon. Petrovsky had remained in Paris, so we attended to our own bags. After only a brief cab ride through the heart of the city, we finally fetched-up at a great hotel, called La Normandy, situated nicely on the main Boulevard, near the Casino and in sight of the great beach and Channel, which are the main attractions of the place. There was no time that evening to find Radine, so, of course, Montclaire and I made do with the entertainment provided by the Casino. Picot meanwhile visited the local gendarmerie, where he conscripted two of their lads to accompany us the next day.

After breakfast the next morning, we and our gendarmes took cabs to a small villa that lay nearby, in the Rue Raspail. The housekeeper, who answered our knock with a jaundiced eye, moved quickly to consult her employer and then admitted us to a study, where we found Radine.

He was nothing like I had imagined. No balding dome of a head, no scholarly slouch to his shoulders, no erudite manner to his speech. Instead, we found a tall, slender man of middle years with jet black hair, finely made features, and a neatly trimmed beard. He wore a smoking jacket and after brief introductions, greeted us warmly.

"Ah, gentlemen. Come in. Come in, by all means. Please join me around the hearth. Hettie will bring café noir in a few moments I am sure. In the meantime, I know you have important business that brings you to my door. A mutual friend has already alerted me, you see."

Radine offered us cigars from his box, and as we all stoked-up and let waft a generous cloud of smoke into the Professor's study, Montclaire explained our business in detail.

"Oh yes," Radine exclaimed, "You wish to know about *The Tears of Buddha*, eh?"

Just then, the housekeeper arrived with our coffee, and so we each took a cup to sip, along with our cigars.

"There is a saying about those bowls that you may not know, but which is often repeated by those who are fascinated by them."

"What is that?" asked Picot.

"It is said that they are almost always out of the sight but that they appear in times of tragedy and distress."

"That is certainly the present case," Montclaire sighed. "This time they are the harbingers of death — the death of a young woman."

Radine's eyes saddened. "Yes, I have heard. The daughter of old Pierre Joffre."

"I say, you are well informed," said Montclaire. "What else do you know of the bowls?"

"Perhaps. I make it my business to be well informed of such things. Within the bounds of the law, that is," he rushed to say, smiling at Picot.

"So pleased to see you again, by the way, Picot."

The young detective merely nodded.

"Nevertheless…," Radine returned to his subject.

We fell into an uneasy silence, as the professor took a sip of his coffee and then drew on his cigar.

"Nevertheless, what?" Montclaire finally asked.

"Well, there is the small matter, first, of the price of the information. After all, it too is a commodity, and I find myself in possession of something quite valuable."

"How much?" Montclaire pressed.

"10,000FF."

"*D'accord.*"

"Your word is good, Montclaire, but your cheque is even better. These are evil times, and one hardly knows whom to trust, you see."

Montclaire went to Radine's nearby desk, took up paper and pen, and hurriedly wrote out the draft upon his bank."

Radine took the scrap, smiled, and tucked it in his inside pocket. "Look to the dealer, Dulac. He has them," the professor said with absolute confidence. "He has just told a buyer for the German Kaiser's personal collection that he can obtain the bowls. That is my information and it is as good as your cheque, Montclaire." He smiled again.

I tried not to let on, but I had not expected Radine to name Dulac. I had all along assumed that Dulac — a pink little man who seemed so earnest and whose reputation as an art dealer was pristine, could not be our thief. And now, both Montclaire and Picot were prepared to accept Radine's accusation as verified truth. I remained skeptical.

Montclaire refused to linger another night in Deauville, and so we hurried to put ourselves on the afternoon train to Paris. In the peaceful rocking of our carriage, I put it to Montclaire, "So the Kaiser is in this business, after all?"

"It would seem so," he agreed. "He is an avid collector, mainly on behalf of the Museum in Berlin, but for his own family as well. The bowls are just the sort of thing — the mystique you might say — that would attract his interest. I might even say, his *avarice*."

"If Radine's information is accurate, how will we force Dulac to confess?" Picot wondered. "He is an important man. He has important friends and resources, after all. Not the sort of person you can nab on the street and throw into La Santé."

Montclaire's jaw stiffened and his eyes narrowed. "Picot, that is exactly what I want you to do. Tomorrow morning, you and some gendarmes are going to drag Dulac from his office and off to La Santé, and I want you to hold him there on my warrant and under an anonymous name."

"Hold him?" Picot gasped. "His family and friends are going to raise bloody hell with the Minister. His lawyers will be all over us both when they find out what has happened. And, they *will* find out, you know."

"I know. But it will take them a few days, and in that time Dulac will have an opportunity to consider his situation, and his guilty conscience will assert itself. When the time comes, we'll sweat him and, if I have to, I'll...."

Montclaire stopped himself in mid-sentence, knowing that what he was about to say would shock both Picot and me. As the young detective and I exchanged glances, I knew for certain, and I suppose Picot suspected, that Montclaire was capable of... well, he was capable even of violence. I had long-since come to know that Montclaire was not entirely sane and I did not like to see his violent nature raise its head in this matter, but I also knew that the image of Marie-Claire's bloody body and the bloody little girl had seized Montclaire and had engaged whatever it was within him that was capable of the most horrific violence. It seemed to me he was in the grip of a smoldering rage and I feared how it might assert itself.

Our train arrived in the late evening, and as we parted from Picot, Montclaire reminded. "When you arrest Dulac tomorrow morning, Picot, make sure that it is done without a scene. Take him away to prison quietly."

"As you say, Monsieur," Picot said with conviction. "It will be done discreetly."

# Chapter Twelve
## The Prisoner in La Santé

We heard nothing from Picot until next afternoon when Petrovsky brought a terse note that read: "All done as you ordered."

Montclaire smiled faintly to read the note, and then returned to his library where exciting researches concerning the evolution of the ancient French phrase *bellezour anima* into its modern form were at a delicate stage. Assured that I would eventually learn the outcome, I decided to pay a much-needed visit to the Albion Club, where a few of my chums from the old regiment were negotiating the equally tricky issue of whether Bonnie Rouge or Potentate would win the Grand Steeplechase de Paris at Auteuil. When I returned to Number 6 later that evening, I found Montclaire in a hot dispute with two of his friends from the Sorbonne on the reliability of a strange, medieval document called the *Séquence Eulalia*. Fascinating as the debate sounded — I could hear shouting through the thick doors of Montclaire's study — I decided to forego the opportunity to participate in favor of finding an early bed.

Thereafter, for the next three days, Picot reported to Montclaire every morning on the state of the prisoner in La Santé and on the concern among Dulac's friends that he had gone missing. By the third morning, Picot could attest that, except the fretting Brouillard, who Montclaire often referred to as Monsieur Le pisse-au-lit (Mr. Bedwetter), no one was yet aware of Dulac's whereabouts. Montclaire decided it was time to confront the old thief and to "wring the truth from him." I didn't like the sound of that last part, because I knew how bloody-minded Montclaire could be in such matters, but as we drove across Paris to the Prison, accompanied by Picot, I convinced myself that Dulac would likely confess without much 'wringing.'

The chief warden of La Santé met us at the drab front entrance and guided us through a rabbit's warren of narrow passages, up several flights of narrow stairs, and into a maze of small rooms, with bare walls, rough-made chairs, and thick oak doors. As we sat in one such room, the warden went to fetch our prisoner.

In a short while, Dulac arrived, with a guard at each elbow. Dressed all in the drab uniform of prison gray and red-eyed from sleeplessness and weeping, the little blister reminded me of a wilted chrysanthemum. As the guards propped him up, he drooped noticeably and then exhaled a deep sigh upon seeing Montclaire. The guards sat him in a chair facing us and they remained with a hand on each of his shoulders.

"Dulac, we are on to your thievery," said Montclaire with a hard look and a menacing voice. "The only question now is to find out why you killed the girl."

At that last, Dulac's eyes bulged and his mouth fell agape.

"Murder! I didn't kill her. No, no, no!" he whined. Then with a hand on each temple, he began to rock back and forth in his chair, repeating over and over, "No. No. No."

It seemed to me that he was falling into a delirium and I fully expected him to drop to the floor in a dead faint at any moment. But the guards steadied him and there he sat, stone-cold rigid, staring at Montclaire in frozen anguish.

"If you are not the murderer, Dulac, then perhaps you'll want to tell me what happened," said Montclaire, now with calm sympathy in his voice and eyes.

Dulac seemed to resonate to Montclaire's more *sympatique* persona. His shoulders relaxed and he breathed a deep sigh of relief. Or, was it merely exhaustion?

"Oh yes. I must tell you," he said, closing his eyes in apparent resignation.

"I took the bowls, but I didn't kill the girl. You must believe me!" he pleaded.

"Go on," Montclaire said, his voice as cold as the crypt.

"I was to meet her at ten o'clock, at her flat. She did not want anyone to see me arrive, I guessed because her family was sensitive about the sale. People are that way, you know."

Montclaire leaned back in his chair. "Yes, I know how people are."

"Well, I arrived and there was no answer to my knock. So, I left. As I drove in my cab toward home, I decided to turn around and see if she had not returned home. Still, time to make our arrangements, you see, and I was eager to close the sale."

"Yes, I see," said Montclaire.

"I guess it was near eleven-thirty o'clock when I knocked at her door again, and there was still no answer. I don't know why, but I decided to try the door and to my surprise, it opened. I peered inside and noticed a lamp was burning in the sitting room, just off the foyer. So, I went in and when I looked through the door of the sitting room...."

He gasped, closed his eyes, drew a deep breath, and then put his hands to his mouth. It seemed to me that the memory was going to make him vomit.

"Steady-on," Montclaire encouraged, taking a flask from his pocket and handing it to Dulac. The little bounder swilled a generous gulp of brandy and then continued.

"Merci, Monsieur. As I was saying, I peered into the sitting room and there I saw the body. It was a bloody mess if ever I imagined one, though I never in my life imagined that a murdered woman could look like that. It was beyond awful," he said shaking his head. "Her eyes looking at me." He shuddered and closed his eyes.

"You are right," I agreed. "My sentiments exactly."

"Go on," said Montclaire.

"I remember that I gagged to see it, but I did not throw up. I don't know why. I turned away and it was then that I saw the baby, crawling about the floor, asking for her mamma."

Reminded of the sad image, Montclaire winced and then shifted in his chair.

"It was then that the thought that I might find the bowls occurred to me. I started searching, first in the sitting room and then in the bedroom. I tripped over furniture and made a frightful noise. There, in the drawer of an armoire, I found a box and in the box... there, in the box were the bowls. *The Tears of Buddha.*"

"And you decided to take them, assuming that everyone would think the woman was murdered by someone who wanted them."

"I don't think I was imagining things that clearly, Monsieur. I just took them because they are so beautiful and I could not resist having them. I had already found a buyer for them…."

"Yes, we know," Picot interrupted. "A German buyer."

Dulac's eyes left no doubt he was surprised that we knew so much about his business.

"Yes. A buyer. And so I took them. I took up the box and ran out of the apartment. The door banged behind me. I ran down the stairs and into my cab, which I'd paid to wait for me. And that was the end of it, Monsieur. You must believe me. I found the Bernard girl dead and I took the bowls, but I did not kill her. I did not kill her," he repeated and then put his face in his hands and began to weep.

Montclaire glanced at me and then at Picot, but no one spoke for a long moment. Montclaire took the flask from his pocket once again and nudged Dulac's shoulder with it.

"Here. Have another," he said, as the little man looked up. Dulac took the flask and once again took a generous swill.

Montclaire leaned back in his chair, lit a cigarette, and drew on it for a few minutes. Picot and I sat quietly, as Dulac continued to rock nervously in his chair, often with his eyes closed.

"I believe you, Monsieur Dulac," Montclaire finally said. "I don't want to believe you, but I do, somehow. Now, however, you must take us to the bowls and show us where you have hidden them."

Dulac agreed heartily to do so, I supposed for no better reason than to spend a few hours in the fresh air and sunlight. He directed us to his gallery and shop, in the neighborhood of Saint-Germain-des-Prés. At the back of his shop there stood a tall safe and from it, Dulac drew a box. We took the box to a nearby table and, for some reason, all paused before opening it. I suppose to prepare ourselves to finally see the objects we'd heard so much about.

Inside, three beautiful little bowls rested in their velvet nests. To me, they all appeared to be identical, and as Dulac lifted one out of the box and held it up to the light, I could see that it was flawless. I'm no aficionado of Chinese crockery, but even I could readily see the reason for all the gasping about the bowls. They were certainly beautiful and, though each had swirls of colors in the porcelain, they were all the same. *How had that happened*, I wondered?

Dulac replaced the bowl. Montclaire closed the box and handed it to Picot.

"For now, we'll keep this in the Sûreté's vault. Tell no one, including Monsieur Joffre, that we have recovered the bowls."

Then Montclaire turned to Dulac.

"If you tell anyone that I have these bowls, I will castrate you." He said it with such easy nonchalance — like announcing he would purchase a new hat — that no one would have failed to believe him. I could tell by his face that Dulac believed.

Picot nodded and took the box. He also returned Dulac to La Santé, on a new charge of art theft and permitted him to have contact with his lawyer. I have never been certain how it happened, but later he was released without trial and somehow returned to his business with no apparent stain on his reputation. Though I was chagrined that he had escaped justice, I took some satisfaction that Montclaire had exacted a price from him.

Our discovery that Dulac had purloined the bowls from Marie-Claire's flat, stepping over her body to do so, dispirited me and I told Montclaire so.

"Here we have been hot on the scent of whoever took those bowls, assuming that he had killed Marie-Claire to get them, and now — dash it! — we learn that this business is *not* about those bloody bowls at all!"

"Yes, we had one beautiful possibility in front of us and now, by hard work, we have proved that it was not true. And so, the truth must lie elsewhere."

I had expected Montclaire to share my disappointment, but I found that my rant had merely caused him to smile.

"Fitz, there is no tool in the detective's kit more powerful than the law of elimination. It does its work perfectly and remorselessly, and it takes no notice of our feelings."

# Chapter Thirteen
## "The Gambler King"

As I expected, Montclaire and Picot now fell back mainly on the assumption that Marie-Claire had somehow become entangled in the problems of her brother, Georges, and had been murdered for her trouble. Georges was still missing and assumed to have been taken and perhaps killed by the gambling syndicate that he had crossed.

For my part, I continued to be troubled by that attempt on Montclaire's life during the evening we had met Mademoiselle Claude and what roused my curiosity most was that the assassin was German. That seeded in my mind the idea that this was somehow an issue that involved the Germans and the one thing that intrigued me most was that Dulac's customer for the bowls was the German Kaiser. We had learned by sad experience what a murderous fellow Kaiser Wilhelm could be, especially when someone stood in the way of something he had set his mind to have.

Montclaire once again retreated into his own occupations, apparently waiting for some element of the investigation to mature or to present an opportunity for action. That intervention came more quickly than I had reckoned, and from an unexpected direction.

As I recall, it was two days later that Petrovsky handed Montclaire a small envelope that had arrived in the morning post. It contained an invitation from Monsieur Marcel Reynard, one of the leaders of the Government's majority in the Chamber of Deputies — a close political ally of Brouillard, in fact — and also one of France's wealthiest men. It was said that his fortune derived mainly from his grandfather, who had grown rich as a financial backer of the schemes of Emperor Napoleon III, mainly in North Africa. "Reynard invites us to dine with him this evening at Ledoyen on the Champs-Elysées," said Montclaire, with a puzzled frown.

*Whatever could that be about?* I remember asking myself. Though I imagined several things, I was entirely unprepared for what we learned.

As we alighted from our cab that evening, Reynard's secretary — an elfin chap with a long sallow face — greeted us at the entrance and guided us to a private dining room at the back of the famous restaurant. There, we found the Deputy himself — a smiling rotund man with a moon face and several chins, all of which quivered as he spoke and laughed.

"Welcome gentlemen, he greeted, guiding us to our chairs. "I have taken the liberty of ordering a bit of cognac ahead of our meal if you do not mind."

"Not at all," Montclaire responded, also smiling.

When the waiters had set the table and the secretary had closed the door behind them, I expected Reynard to explain the purpose of his invitation. I was disappointed. Instead, he guided the conversation off into matters of the French political scene and then over such deadly dull topics as funding for France's rail system, the trades union movement, and American investment in France. Things droned on in this fashion in only the way an unforgiving politician could steer them until our dinner was almost over.

"I won't beat any further about the bush, Monsieur," he finally turned earnestly to Montclaire. "I know you are wondering why I have invited you here this evening."

"Indeed, I am," Montclaire agreed. By this time I was so jaded and nearly comatose that I fully expected him to say that it was the situation in North Africa that prompted his invitation.

"It is the matter of the murder of old Joffre's daughter."

That caused me to perk-up. Montclaire too. I'm sure my mouth fell slightly agape to hear it.

"I wish to be of service to your investigation."

"How so?" Montclaire asked, with a cold face that somehow showed no surprise at all.

"By preventing you from going down a path of inquiry that would prove fruitless to yourselves and troubling to others."

"Oh? What path is that? I am always eager to save myself and others some trouble."

Reynard smiled faintly and leaned forward in his chair, offering each of use a cigar.

"*Bien*. I am aware, through my own sources, you understand, that you are concerned that young Georges Joffre found himself in deep trouble because of his gambling debts. And you may be inclined to think that those who held his debts and found it necessary to make an example of him were also somehow involved in the murder of his sister."

Montclaire's eyes narrowed a little, as he took a sip of after-dinner port.

"I am in a position to free you from that concern, Monsieur. To assure you there is absolutely no connection between young Joffre's... creditors, and the young woman's murder," he explained, pounding his index finger on the table three times as he said words 'absolutely no connection.'

"Interesting to know, but precisely how is it that you can give such assurances?" Montclaire asked.

"I am not at liberty to tell you, Monsieur, but I have my sources of information and my friends and they are keen to relieve your mind on that score."

"You mean the gambling syndicate — those powerful men of affairs who control much of the wagering in France, from Dieppe to Nice."

Reynard's face lost its smile and his eyes grew menacing. "We needn't discuss that, Montclaire. No need, you understand. It's enough that I can assure you that those... those 'men of affairs' as you call them have nothing to do with what concerns you and therefore you need not concern yourself with them. Believe me, it is dangerous for you to take further interest in such things. Very dangerous."

"I understand perfectly what you mean, Monsieur. And, of course, your assurance is a valuable thing to have in my pocket, as I proceed."

Reynard had hoped to have more confirmation than that from Montclaire, but he understood that no more would be forthcoming.

"Very well," he sniffed, signaling that our pleasant dinner at Ledoyen had come to a sour conclusion. As we took our leave, he offered one last bit of advice.

"There is no reason to worry further about those gambling debts and those who hold them, eh? It was another matter altogether."

"That would be an interesting thing, Monsieur. Not to worry," said Montclaire, as we left the famous politician in the dining room by himself.

"Merely a matter of collecting their debts from old Joffre, eh? And making an example of his luckless son?" I put it to Montclaire, as our cab moved through the Place Victor Hugo on its way home. "Don't bother to pry into our affairs." I harrumphed.

"I have heard rumors for many years of a powerful man — some call him the King of the Gamblers — who is the force behind virtually all wagering in the country. And now, *mon ami*, I believe we have met him. And we know one very important thing.

"What?"

"He is frightened of our investigation."

"And yet, he tells you to draw-off."

"That was the substance of the message, and make no mistake. Reynard delivered the message with a smile, but it was a threat. You and I could disappear as readily as young Joffre, they mean to say, and they intend me to heed the warning."

"And will you? I mean, do you believe what they say, warning or not? About not being concerned in the murder of Marie-Claire?"

Montclaire smiled. "I dislike being threatened, Fitz. But, what to do? What to do?" he repeated and then fell into a long silence.


As soon as we had returned to the apartment, I said good night and thereafter enjoyed a sound sleep. Montclaire seemed to have no such intention to go to bed, but I had no idea of his plans for the remainder of the evening.

The next morning, still groggy from a profound sleep, I started and then rocked back on my heels to read the headline that screamed from *La Figaro*:

*Deputy Found Dead.*
*Marcel Reynard's Throat Cut, As He Slept.*

# PART THREE

## Lovers and Assassins

# Chapter Fourteen
# Madame Joffre Visits

Montclaire did not speculate about what had happened to Reynard, which gave me a chill to think how the politician had met his fate. And did Reynard's death endanger young Joffre, if indeed he was still alive? I decided not to fret about such things unless they came to play in the solution to Marie-Claire's murder. At that moment, it seemed to me the gambling syndicate was a peripheral matter because they had gone to some difficulty to assure — and threaten — Montclaire that they had nothing to do with the murder. Still, I assumed it mattered some that they coupled their assurance with a threat.

My thoughts quickly returned to a puzzle that we'd never quite dealt with — the attempt on our lives. The assassin who came very close to killing one of us the night we met Mademoiselle Claude. I decided that I would take the first opportunity to press the issue with Montclaire, but that morning I had little time to do so. Almost as soon as we finished breakfast and prepared to go out, an unexpected visitor appeared at our door.

"Madame Joffre, Monsieur," Petrovsky announced, and at the name, Montclaire shot me a quizzical look.

We had not seen Marie-Claire's mother since that first interview with the grieving family. Now, days later, her face remained riven with grief. I am sure she had been crying.

"Welcome Madame," Montclaire greeted, guiding her to a chair. "Here. Take a seat by the hearth. It's a chilly morning."

"Thank you, Monsieur, but my purpose in this visit will not take long," she said, stiffening and composing herself. "I've come to tell you something that I should have told days ago. I did not consider it important at the time, but on reflection, I have decided that it is best to tell. Even if it means nothing."

"Oh? Then, please…," Montclaire encouraged.

"A silly thing, perhaps, but puzzling, and that's why I've decided to speak of it."

Montclaire waited while Madame paused to collect her thoughts and my curiosity rose.

"A week before her death Marie-Claire confided to me that a problem had arisen between her and François. She told me that she had seen him with someone, and when she mentioned it to him offhandedly, he grew quite upset, she said."

"Had she seen him with another woman?" Montclaire asked, indelicately I thought. "Suspected him of being unfaithful, perhaps? Something of that sort?"

"Marie-Claire did not say, so I have no idea. Perhaps. I have considered that myself. A silly thing, I suspect. You know how young lovers are. And now this." She began to tear up and put a handkerchief to one eye.

Once again we paused to allow Madame to compose herself.

"Did Marie-Claire say where this had happened? Where she'd seen François with this other person?"

The question seemed to surprise a little. "Why yes. I'd quite forgotten that until you asked. She said it was in the Bois, at that little park near the entrance to the racecourse. You know the one? With the fountain. Just off the drive that goes between the lakes."

"Yes, I know it well, Madame. An out-of-the-way sort of place."

*Just the sort of place for a discreet assignation*, I imagined.

Montclaire thought for a moment before asking a final question.

"Tell me, have you mentioned this to François at all? Since the... since Marie-Claire's death?"

"Oh no. I did not wish to add to his grief. I'm sure the little spat between the two of them has weighed upon him these past days."

"Yes, of course," said Montclaire. "And in that case, I will ask you to refrain from mentioning it to anyone. Let us keep it just between ourselves for the time being, eh?" he said, taking her hands and patting them.

"Very well, Monsieur. I'll not speak of it."


When Madame Joffre had gone, Montclaire turned suddenly to the very thing I'd been stewing about before the visit.

"I have been forced to return to an issue that begs attention — from that night we were set upon by assassins. It is the question of who knew we were to be there. At the time, you suggested it was Mademoiselle Claude who had entrapped us, and I did not object because it was an obvious suspicion. But, I knew even then that there was another name that we did not take into account — another possibility."

"Oh? What name is that?"

Montclaire's face suddenly grew expressionless. "Picot."

# Chapter Fifteen
# Who Knew?

That was the last name I expected to hear.

"Montclaire, you cannot be suggesting that Picot is suspect. That he had anything to do with the assassination attempt."

"I am not suggesting anything, Fitz, but I do say that he was the one other person who knew we would be in that alley, and what Picot knew may have inadvertently assisted our would-be assassins."

That confused me, as was the case so often when Montclaire's mind was working at the speed of a racing train and mine was ambling along at a leisurely stroll in the park. When I caught up, I asked, "How did Picot inadvertently assist our would-be assassins? Sûreté detectives do not go about babbling about clandestine meetings with criminals."

Montclaire frowned but did not answer. Instead, he ordered Petrovsky to hail a cab.

"*I* cannot answer your question, *mon vieux*, but I'll wager Picot can do so. Let us ask him," he added, in his jaunty way.


We judged that Picot would be found at Sûreté headquarters, near Notre Dame de Paris. The cab ride was a long one and at a time of day when the streets of Paris were always busiest. We arrived in mid-afternoon and it took a while to find our query. We retreated to his office and there Montclaire first brought him up to date on all the Madame Joffre has told.

"And now, Picot, Sir Francis and I have a question to put to you. The answer may well confirm a suspicion that I now have."

"Of course," said Picot. "What?"

"The evening that Fitz and I went to meet Mademoiselle Claude and the assassins made their attempt. Aside from Mademoiselle Claude, only you knew where we would be and when."

Picot's face lost its color. "*Oui.*"

"Whom did you tell of our plan?"

Picot needed only a moment to remember. "Colonel Fleury. I was at the DB that afternoon and during my meeting with Fleury, to bring him up to date on the investigation, of course, I told him of your meeting."

"Only Fleury?" Montclaire pressed. "No other? Not even the Minister — Brouillard?"

"No one," Picot affirmed. "But…."

Picot paused in mid-sentence.

"One other."

"What!"

"When I entered Fleury's office, he was speaking with François Gargal. Yes, Gargal was there."

# Chapter Sixteen
# Egon Renzler

When Picot said that name, somehow it all came into focus for me. Montclaire too, from the look on his face, as he tossed me a quick, knowing look. What I did not know at that point was what Montclaire would make of Picot's testimony.

"Is anyone beyond suspicion, Montclaire?" I insisted. "Why not suspect Fleury?" I added, thinking of any reason to divert suspicion from Gargal, the grieving fiancé.

Montclaire smiled.

"Of course, you are right, Fitz. So, we must have a strategy for both of them. First, however, we will devise a way to relieve Gargal of suspicion, as you obviously wish."

"And what is that? What strategy?" Picot asked.

Montclaire went to Picot's desk, took up pen and paper, and composed a brief note. When he had done so, he handed it to me and I read aloud.

"Must see you. The usual place. Nine o'clock tomorrow evening," it said in bold print.

"There is one problem with this trick, Monsieur," Picot challenged. "Suppose Gargal and his comrade have a form of words that every note must have, else it is an obvious trick?"

"Oui, that is a danger for us. It would be good tradecraft to have a code word that must be in every communication. If they do not, it is sloppy. Let us hope they have been sloppy, or perhaps that receiving a note without the word nonetheless frightens Gargal and he does something stupid."

"Very well," said Picot, dubiously.

"Yes, I know, Picot. Such a strategy is a thin reed, but it is our best hope. We could try to place Gargal under surveillance, but in the present circumstances, he will certainly avoid initiating a meeting with his German contact like he would avoid the plague. Our only hope is to convince him that his contact finds it imperative to meet."

"Should the note be in French? Or German?" I asked. "What language do the two use to communicate? Gargal undoubtedly knows German well. If we get that wrong, Gargal will be warned off."

Montclaire smiled at me sympathetically. "Let us rely upon German arrogance, *mon ami*. We'll assume that a German would not condescend to communicate with a compromised Frenchman in French."

When Montclaire had rewritten the message in German and sealed the note in a small envelope, he handed it to Picot.

"Make sure Gargal finds this note in the letterbox of his apartment this evening. Take no risk. Give it to the postman to deliver with the other letters."


Picot delivered the note exactly as Montclaire had ordered. Then we waited until the following day to put the next phase of our effort into action. We now had every confidence that Major Gargal would either report the strange communication to Fleury or, as Montclaire believed, appear in the Bois the next evening to meet his German contact. By next afternoon, Picot assured us that Fleury had heard nothing from Gargal and so we prepared for our surveillance in the Bois.

That surveillance was easier imagined than done. For one thing, we found few good positions from which to watch the park and fountain, which Madame Joffre had reported as the place where Marie-Claire had observed Gargal's meeting with 'someone.' We decided that the only safe vantage point would be a row of hedges about thirty yards from the fountain, and those hedges provided cover for only the three of us. Montclaire ordered our compliment of gendarmes to hide themselves even further away and await his call to action when the time came.

Expecting Gargal to arrive at nine o'clock, we took up our positions at eight o'clock, laying on our bellies beneath the hedges, and there we used our glasses to observe. I noticed that Montclaire had brought his opera lenses, which somehow struck me as appropriate, for if his strategy proved successful we would surely witness an unfolding drama.

As we waited a light-footed fog began to roll through the little park, which was illuminated by a single gaslight. I wondered if our view of things would be obscured by the thickening mist.

Time passes slowly lying on the ground, in the cold, damp discomfort of a hedgerow. Montclaire permitted no conversation, so we waited in our own thoughts. Shifting from elbow to elbow, I finally concluded we'd been waiting under the hedges for at least an hour, so I consulted my watch. 9:15 pm. Gargal was late if indeed he was coming at all.

Still waiting in silence, I began to muse that if Gargal failed to appear it would be evidence of a sort of his innocence. Or, perhaps it would merely tell that our ruse was too clumsy and ill-conceived to draw him out. That led me to a truly shocking thought. What if Gargal had seen through our ruse, and was even then boarding a train for Switzerland at the Gare de Lyons?

Just as I was certain that our trick had failed, a coach turned into the short drive that led to the fountain. It stopped just short of the gaslight. Its occupant waited aboard.

Montclaire signaled us to remain calm, and so we waited for what seemed like a quarter-hour or more. The coach remained motionless, the occupant unseen. Feeling the chill of the mist, the driver shrank into his greatcoat like a turtle. Soon, he decided the wait would be a long one, and so he lit his pipe.

Somehow Montclaire seemed to take the pipe as a signal to act. He rose suddenly and commenced a mad dash toward the coach, with Picot and me close on his heels. At first, the driver did not see us approaching, but when he caught sight of us he whipped-up in a frenzied attempt to escape. Before he could turn and get underway, however, Picot had jumped on the starboard horse and stopped him, while Montclaire opened the door. A dangerous move, because whoever was inside might have been waiting with a cocked pistol.

Just as he did so, however, the occupant jumped from the door on the other side and sprinted across the open park, toward the race-course gates, in the fog. Montclaire circled the coach and ran after the fleeing man. As I pursued, I saw both of them disappear in the fog ahead of me. Meanwhile, Picot blew his whistle to summon the gendarmes.

In such conditions, I was sure Montclaire would lose his prey, but then I heard noises, ran toward them, and found that Montclaire had tackled Gargal — in the finest tradition of Harrow football — and the two were wrestling on the ground. Suddenly, Gargal slipped Montclaire's grasp and jumped to his feet, a knife glinting in his hand. I drew my Webley to shoot the foul blister, but Montclaire must have glimpsed my hand and shouted, "No, Fitz! Don't shoot him!"

Just then Gargal glanced at me, and that was his undoing. Montclaire — a master of that strange form of foot pugilism the French call *savate* — jumped to his feet and, in the next instant, kicked Gargal full in the side of his head. In all my experience with the grisly matter of war and battlefields, I have never known a more ruthless hand-to-hand blood-spiller than Montclaire. Thereafter, it was a matter of pummeling Gargal to near unconsciousness, as Picot, the gendarmes, and I stood by, observing by the light of Picot's torch, and wincing a little at the blood that now poured freely from Gargal's nose, mouth, and ear.

I thought Montclaire intended to show no mercy and would con-tinue beating his captive to a jelly, but Picot ran at Montclaire and pulled him away.

The gendarmes joined Picot's effort and together they saved Gargal from Montclaire by dragging him to his feet, while Picot held both arms around Montclaire to prevent him from resuming his work on the Major. I could see Montclaire had already done some damage to Gargal.

"The Major will need care," I shouted to Picot, who knew immediately what to do.

"To the coach," he ordered the gendarmes, "and then to the Ursulines" — a nearby *Infermerie* operated by the nuns of the Ursuline Convent.

There was little congestion in the streets at that hour, and so we arrived at the *Infermerie* within the half-hour. Once there, it took the sisters an hour to revive Gargal to consciousness and to bandage his wounds. Montclaire continued to show no mercy. He started the interrogation of his prisoner immediately.

"You are a traitor and a murderer, Major. You are now bound for the guillotine," he shouted in Gargal's bloody face. The only thing that will save you from that fate is to tell me all. Leave no fact unsaid, for I promise if you do you will surely have the knife."

Gargal's face, such as it was, lighted with the prospect of sparing himself that miserable death.

"Do you mean to say you will spare me if I tell you all I know? You swear it?" he pleaded, wincing through the pain of speaking.

"Yes," said Montclaire, "I promise you."

Gargal did not hesitate to begin his effort to save himself.

"Ask me what you will then," he whispered in resignation. "I'll hold nothing back."

"When did you choose to betray your country, Major, and why?" Montclaire asked, a frigid tone in his voice.

"Two years ago, as we began to make progress against the German code. I knew Berlin would pay handsomely to know what I could tell them. Marie-Claire had told me everything."

"Because she loved you and trusted you. You vile monster!" Picot shouted.

"Why? Why did you do it?" Montclaire asked, calmly.

Gargal jolted, as a spasm of pain hit his neck. Then he continued.

'I needed money... to pay... to pay my debts. I had borrowed, first from my bank and then from loan sharks, to invest in the Bourse — in a company in Egypt. I lost everything. The loan sharks were going to kill me unless I paid in thirty days. I tried to borrow more, but failed and so...." He shook his head and then coughed up some blood. A sister wiped it from his cheek.

"...and so you sold out your country, you son-of-a-whore," Picot shouted, lunging at Gargal. I reached swiftly to catch his forearm and then pulled him back before he could deliver Gargal another blow to the head.

When things had once again returned to calm, Montclaire said, "Go on."

"I grew more desperate, you see, as it became inevitable the loan sharks would kill me to make an example. Or, they would ruin my career... if the DB found out about it. I was trapped, either way... with no way out. No way out, but one."

He paused to gather his thoughts or nerve, and then to spit up some blood.

"You may think it was easy. Easy for me to... to betray my country, but it wasn't. I agonized, and then I saw it was the only way. I was desperate I tell you!" he shouted, and then clutching at Montclaire's hand.

Montclaire drew it back. "Continue."

"I knew from my work that the Austrian Embassy is a beehive of German espionage. Most of the Under-Secretaries there are, in fact, German agents."

He paused again, this time to draw a deep, painful breath.

"So I made contact and waited for them to respond. They did so quickly. The negotiations were brief. They gave me all I needed to pay off my creditors... to save myself. Don't you see?"

"And what did you give them in exchange?" Picot asked. "To save yourself."

"At first, very little. Things that I figured they already knew. But then they began to ask questions about very sensitive matters... because they knew my Section at the DB, you see."

He took another deep breath, and winced, clutching at his side. Montclaire, I supposed, had broken a rib or two.

"Finally, I tried to refuse them, but they wouldn't hear of it. They threatened to expose me. So, I revealed everything I knew of our code-breaking work... all I knew of Marie-Claire and her work and her success also. They were pleased."

"I imagine they were," said Montclaire, his voice laced with sarcasm. "You gave them the crown jewels."

"Why did you murder Marie-Claire?" Picot asked suddenly, and to hear it, Gargal gasped.

"I didn't kill her!" he insisted. "That was... that was the Germans."

"How did it happen? That the Germans killed her?" Montclaire continued.

"One day she chanced to see me... in the Bois... meeting with my contact."

Montclaire glanced at me.

"She mentioned it to me later and it surprised me. I was caught off-guard and I reacted badly — stupidly. It unnerved me to know she'd seen me. I began to wonder. What if it aroused her suspicions? What if she said something to Fleury? We were always being encouraged to report anything suspicious or unusual. What if she reported it, I began to worry? It drove me crazy; don't you see? Crazy!"

"Go on," Montclaire said, in a toneless voice.

"I decided I must tell my contact. Ask what to do."

"Once again to save yourself, eh?" said Picot.

"Yes," Gargal closed his eyes. "Yes, to save myself."

"Who was this contact?" asked Montclaire, leaning-in.

"Renzler. Egon Renzler is his name. He is a native Austrian but in the Kaiser's employ. He is a senior agent of the Geheime Nachreichtendienst der Heeres."

Montclaire shot me a significant glance, as Gargal once again began to weep and wipe his eyes with his shirtsleeve. Then he coughed up more blood, clutching his chest in pain. When he recovered, he continued to weep.

"Don't you see," he pleaded. "Renzler explained that we couldn't chance it. That it was my life or...."

He stopped himself in mid-sentence.

"...or, Marie-Claire's. You traded her life for yours," Montclaire finished the thought for him. "So it was Renzler who murdered Marie-Claire... to make sure?"

"Yes. Among his other talents, Renzler is a well-trained assassin. A brutal man. He enjoys his work."

*Rather like Montclaire*, I sighed to myself.

"Yes. I've seen his work," said Montclaire, dryly.

Then, in a calculated cruelty, Montclaire asked. "Did you know Renzler raped Marie-Claire before he killed her?"

Gargal gasped and then shuddered. He tried to rise, but then fell back on his pillow, screaming incoherently. The sisters rushed in to quiet him and to reassure — to soothe him somehow. It took them a full ten minutes to calm their patient, who, however, continued to weep."

Just then, another of the sisters came to change the bandage on Gargal's cheek, which had been bleeding. In all the commotion, Montclaire lit a cheroot and nonchalantly busied himself with his thoughts. When the bandaging was changed and Gargal had calmed himself, Montclaire continued.

"How do you arrange to meet with Renzler?"

Gargal paused, knowing this was his last chance of a bargain with Montclaire. That the last thing of value he had to give-up was Renzler.

"You swear I will not face the guillotine, Montclaire? You swear it?"

"Yes. I have already given you my word," Montclaire insisted, indignant that Gargal would question his word.

"I leave a note in the lavatory at the Café Toulouse, in Montparnasse. To be authentic, the message in the note must use the word '*tout*.'"

Montclaire's face grew puzzled.

"Did you have a codeword when he contacted you? How did my note to you succeed?"

"Yes. A code. His messages to me had to include the number '9.' Your note did, and so I assumed it was genuine."

I looked at Montclaire and then rolled my eyes heavenward. He smiled.

Gargal continued. "The lavatory is checked daily, in the evening."

"Where do you place the note?"

"On top of a cabinet in the lavatory. No one would look there who did not expect to find something."

Just then, a sister came in with a tray of medications for Gargal. Montclaire ordered Picot to keep a guard on him while he was in the care of the sisters, and then to take him to La Santé, where he was to be kept in strict seclusion. "No visitors and under a false name," Montclaire cautioned.

Before we left, however, Montclaire asked one of the sisters to bring pen and paper and he then instructed Gargal to write to his dictation:

*Must see you. Eight o'clock tomorrow morning.*
*Usual place. All is at risk.*

Gargal's hand was shaky, but he managed to do a passable job. The note, of course, included the all-important code word, '*tout*.' Gargal assured us again that Renzler would know the "usual place" to mean the little park in the Bois.

As we descended the steps of the Convent Infermerie, I could tell Montclaire would waste no time in luring Renzler to the same fate as Gargal. Maybe worse, I figured. Time was critical, for at any moment, Renzler might discover that Gargal had disappeared and then go underground himself.

Montclaire ordered Picot to see that the note was placed in the lavatory the next afternoon, and we would then prepare to meet Renzler the following day.


That same afternoon, Colonel Fleury and Brouillard answered Montclaire's summons to our apartment, where he proposed to brief the two on all that had happened with Gargal. Brouillard, anxious as ever, was in a particular flutter about the murder of his colleague, Marcel Reynard. Montclaire sympathized, and then also told the two of our planned meeting with Renzler. In that regard, he demanded the assurance of the Minister that he could charge Renzler with Marie-Claire's murder and submit him to French justice — that is, to the guillotine.

Brouillard did not hesitate to give his assurance, which pleased Fleury and eased Montclaire's concern. When the Minister had gone, Montclaire laid his plan to entrap Renzler. At the end of it, he told us, Renzler would disappear from all traces on this earth, into a secret trial and execution. It was all to happen within a few days, and so Picot was burdened with preparations, including notifying the judges of France's criminal court who had previously presided at such secret tribunals. The proof to convict him would be Gargal's confession and, most important, Renzler's response to our summons. As I listened to these preparations, I was astounded to learn that there were such things as Secret Tribunals in France, but then a sense of the reality of affairs unclouded my mind — or should I say banished my naïveté — and it seemed entirely reasonable that state should choose to settle some affairs in secret, out the public gaze. In almost the same thought, I wondered if the British Government employed a similar procedure.

We arrived at the park in the Bois the next morning, well before eight o'clock, having posted gendarmes on foot at a safe but useful distance. Montclaire, Picot, and I sat in Gargal's coach, with the window curtains drawn. The coach was driven by Gargal's usual *coachée*, who Montclaire had bribed well for his service. All was, to the best of our ability, just as Renzler would expect to find it.

Unlike Gargal, who had been late, Renzler's coach drew up at the fountain in the park at precisely eight o'clock. There followed a long wait, I supposed, as he assured himself that all was as it should be. I peeked through the curtain in time to see a tall, thin man in a dark suit and fedora alight from the nearby coach. He looked side-to-side as he walked, slowly, cautiously toward us.

"He's coming," I whispered and then drew a deep breath. Soon we heard the sound of footsteps upon the gravel of the drive. He stopped and suddenly there was no sound at all. My heart stopped and I was aware that the only thing that prevented it bounding out of my mouth was my front teeth. I dared not look out to see what the matter was. Just then, however, the footsteps resumed, and almost as quickly there came the sound of someone turning the handle on the coach door. When suddenly the door opened, a dark man with a large black moustache and wearing pince-nez found Montclaire's cocked pistol square in his face. The pince-nez jumped from his nose, but beyond that, he remained as motionless as a corpse.

"Move one muscle without my permission and you are dead," Montclaire said, a tone in his voice as serious as death itself.

"Raise your hands."

The dark man did so, without hesitation. Just then, Picot began to blow his whistle.

I don't know why Picot calculated it was time to blow his whistle, but to Renzler it seemed to be the signal to bolt. He slammed the door. His fedora flew backward as he dashed across the park, in generally the same direction as Gargal had tried to escape. Rather than shoot him, Montclaire dropped his pistol and pursued, and just as with Gargal, Picot and I followed.

Ahead of us, I could see that Renzler could not out run Montclaire. Though he had a start, Montclaire caught him, but just as he approached Renzler turned, a pistol in his hand. Eyes wild, like those of a cornered wolf, the assassin meant to make his stand.

Montclaire stopped short, aware that he had dropped his weapon. It was then I drew the Webley from my inside pocket and, before Montclaire could stop me, I shot the blighter on the run. I had fired three shots. As I learned later, only one had found its mark.

Renzler's pistol fired wide of its mark, and turning, he dropped it and staggered toward the lake. But only a few steps on, he fell to the ground, clutching his leg and screaming like a lost soul. I had hit him, as it turned out, clean through his right knee.

Picot and the gendarmes arrived as if from nowhere, and suddenly Renzler was surrounded, which seemed to make him scream and cry all the more. I'd never shot someone in the knee before, so it was an awakening of sorts to see how painful it was.

Our wounded assassin could stand no questioning at that moment. His wound was too painful. Montclaire ordered the coach to be brought up. The gendarmes dragged Renzler to the coach and tossed him in the front seat, all the while holding his knee and yowling like a stepped-on puppy. As we had with Major Gargal, Montclaire ordered the driver to make for the *Infermerie* of the Ursulines as fast as possible.

Once out on the Rue de la Pompe and heading south at speed, however, the usual mid-morning congestion of wagons, coaches, and carriages on the street began to slow our progress. Suddenly, an overturned wagon in front of us forced us to stop altogether. We came to a halt beside a carriage filled with elderly, fashionably-dressed ladies, clearly out for a pleasant drive. As we sat motionless beside them, Renzler continued to scream and beg for God's mercy, such that the women began to look at us, frown, talk amongst themselves, and I am sure concluded that we were murdering someone in our coach. I tried to mollify their concerns by tipping my hat, waving, and smiling at them in my most charming way. I even gave one old darling the glad eye but to no avail. I was relieved when we finally resumed our drive to the Ursulines.

Not ten minutes later, we fetched-up at the Convent steps. The head sister of the *Infermerie*, who had greeted us at the door several days earlier, gave me a certain look as we carried Renzler, still screaming of course, through the entrance. An obvious expert at the unspoken message, the old nun frowned at me as if I were something that didn't smell quite right — a look that was intended to tell me that this had better be the last bleeding criminal we dragged past her door.

The nuns sent for a nearby physician who arrived within the hour. Meanwhile, they knew what to do to stop Renzler's bleeding and examine the wound. One told me she feared his leg would need to be amputated and that infection was a danger. I did my level best to appear concerned. Picot made some untranslatable French noises that sounded like genuine disappointment and sympathy. *Dash it*, I thought to myself. *The French are so much better at feigning sympathy than are we British.*

# Chapter Seventeen
## Montclaire's Rage

We were forced to leave Renzler in the care of the sisters, with a guard of gendarmes that was at least twice that which Picot had posted for Gargal. Two days later, we learned that Renzler's leg had been amputated above the knee, but that he was out of danger of serious infection.

Like Gargal, after several weeks, Renzler was taken to La Santé under an alias identity and there he remained in strict seclusion, as Montclaire made arrangements through the Minister of Justice, the Tribunal de Police, and the Cour d'Assises — the last being the court in France which tried cases of the death penalty and the one court from which there was no appeal. Montclaire meant to march Renzler to the guillotine as quickly as possible.

All the while that Renzler was in the Infermerie, Montclaire and Picot assembled their case against him, mainly by taking detailed testimony from Gargal and Fleury that would be presented to the court as documentary evidence. There soon arose the thorny issue of whether or not Renzler was to be allowed a lawyer and whether he would be allowed to call witnesses on his behalf. He was granted counsel but not witnesses, and Montclaire seemed satisfied that the trial would proceed quickly to its inevitable conclusion.

In a few days, the trial was placed on the docket of the Cour d'Assises and all was ready. Three days in advance of the trial, however, a grim-faced Brouillard appeared at our door, accompanied by Colonel Fleury. From the start, I could tell that the unexpected visit troubled Montclaire, who nonetheless greeted the pair with his usual cheerfulness.

When we were all seated around the library hearth, awaiting a tray of brandy from Petrovsky, the Minister launched into the explanation for his visit.

"I have news concerning the Renzler affair, Montclaire. News that you will not like."

"Oh?" said Montclaire, raising an eyebrow and reaching for his cigar case.

"The Government — in particular, the Prime Minister and the Minister of War — have decided against a trial."

The news fell like a grenade in the middle of our library. Montclaire was on his feet in an instant.

"What! I hope, Minister, that you mean we are going to take Renzler to the guillotine without benefit of a legal ceremony."

"No, it does not mean that. Not at all. And I don't mind telling you that I argued against what the Prime Minister has decided."

It was then that Fleury spoke up, to explain what had happened.

"It's the Germans, Montclaire. They know we have Renzler, of course, or they suspect it anyway, and they have made the Government an offer. A very surprising offer."

"What?" Montclaire asked, clearly anxious.

"They will exchange three French operatives they have had in custody for more than a year for Renzler. Pure and simple. Three for one."

Brouillard added.

"The Prime Minister, and especially Fleury's boss, the Minister of War, decided that they could not refuse such an offer. No matter Renzler's crimes, the prospect of getting three of ours back was too good to pass up. *Et voilà!*"

Brouillard meant to convey that the Government was going to brook no opposition or argument from Montclaire or anyone. It was a *fait accompli.*


Montclaire waited until Brouillard and Fleury had gone to become furious. His anger, which amounted to a shouted oath that he would never again accept a commission to act as examining magistrate, ended abruptly when he locked himself in his study and there descended into a drunken funk that lasted two days. When he emerged, looking like he'd just made a two-week trek through West Africa; his anger had abated and was replaced by another focus. Gargal.

"There is still the matter of Gargal, Fitz. The matter of what to do with him."

I was surprised that Gargal was still an open matter.

"Prison, of course. Or, transportation. You assured him that if he cooperated he would escape the guillotine."

"Still, there must be a trial. We must satisfy the forms of justice. I must finish my mandate as *juge d'instruction*, eh?"

"Yes, of course," I agreed, not knowing what precisely Montclaire had in mind. But when he then smiled, I sighed inwardly.

# Chapter Eighteen
## "I lied to you"

Montclaire persuaded the Cour d'Assises to replace the Renzler trial on its docket with the trial of Major François Gargal. That was easily done and the Government, I supposed as amends for its shabby behavior in the Renzler matter, conceded to every demand that Montclaire made for the trial.

The single judge who heard the case had reviewed all the evidence carefully and, in as much as Gargal had confessed, quickly accepted the fact of Gargal's guilt, as Montclaire had charged. Gargal's attorney offered no witness to prove his client's innocence.

Upon the day of his sentencing Gargal stood before the same judge, who pronounced: "Monsieur, you will be returned to La Prison de la Santé, and there, on the 14th of this month, you will be executed by guillotine. Such is the will of the French people."

Gargal turned, his eyes bulging and mouth agog, to see Montclaire standing behind him.

"But Monsieur," he stammered, incredulous, "you promised that if I cooperated with you, I would not face the guillotine. What is this? Your word, Monsieur, as a gentleman."

"Oh, that is easily explained, Major," said Montclaire with complete nonchalance. "I lied to you. I always lie to traitors and criminals. Surely, it is a fault of mine, and if you insist that it is a stain on my reputation as a gentleman, well, you will be vindicated. Nonetheless, Major, you will go to the guillotine and I will march you to the scaffold myself."

Gargal then began to rave so incoherently that I did not understand all of his French, but I could tell that he was damning Montclaire to hell.

# Chapter Nineteen
# The Laughing Girl

Three weeks after Gargal met his fate in the courtyard of La Santé, just as I concluded we'd heard to last of the sad affair of Marie-Claire Bernard, visitors arrived, whom I learned Montclaire had invited. Madame Joffre and Sophie, Marie-Claire's sister, followed Petrovsky into the sitting room and in her arms, Sophie carried the baby girl whose appearance at the scene of her mother's murder had so unnerved me. The baby's name, as we learned, was Anne. Now, however, Anne was jolly and laughing. Montclaire, delighted to see them, and especially the child, took the little girl immediately to his knee to bounce and giggle.

Just then, Petrovsky returned, this time with old Professor Baladeur of the Sorbonne *en train*, looking as wizened as ever and plainly a little confused. I hoped for the sake of the child that he would not launch into another discourse on the hated Taipings.

The Joffre ladies said that Georges had not been killed by the gamblers, after all, and had been ransomed after negotiations and the payment of a large sum of money. Money which we supposed the family could ill afford to pay.

After refreshments and a bit of idle chitchat, Montclaire announced a surprise that would surely lighten the hearts of our guests. He walked to the great mahogany cabinet in his sitting room and from it drew a box. When he had placed the box on the table, he opened it to show the three bowls.

"Oh, Monsieur," Madame Joffre gasped, as the baby laughed and giggled. "You've found them! How can we thank you?"

The old Professor, speechless, staggered to the table, his eyes riveted on the bowls. When he finally looked up at Montclaire, however, I could see that he had begun to weep.

# Chapter Twenty
# The Exchange

The negotiation to exchange Egon Renzler for the three French agents took much longer than at first expected, and so it was nine months after the conclusion of Montclaire's investigation and the execution of Gargal that the agreement was finally reached. The exchange took place at a small, village railway station near Zurich. Montclaire insisted on witnessing the actual event. Unable to persuade him otherwise, I told myself that seeing the denouement of his investigation and the return of three Frenchmen might help Montclaire gain a sense of closure and reconcile him finally to the loss of Renzler.

Montclaire did not want to be part of the exchange and so we arrived by an earlier train. We stood on the platform nearby as the small French delegation arrived at that village station that cold morning in October. The train from Paris jolted to a hissing stop and in the smoke I could at first recognize Picot and Fleury, and after them, a man on a crutch descended from the carriage with great difficulty. It was Renzler.

As the train moved on into the station, we could see, across the tracks, on the opposing platform, a delegation of German uniforms, surrounding three hapless civilians. *Those must be the French agents*, I concluded.

At the appointed signal, the two delegations crossed the tracks, Renzler stumbling once as he struggled on his crutch and artificial limb. *At least the blighter didn't leave France a whole man,* I comforted myself, as the exchange was made. When Renzler found himself safely in the hands of his countrymen, however, he turned suddenly to look back. From the opposing platform and leaning on his crutch, he glared at Montclaire and then gave a faint smile.

I worried that Renzler's triumphant gesture would send Montclaire into another spiral of rage, but I was quickly reassured. Montclaire's face remained stone-cold, and in the weeks that followed the exchange, he gave no indication that the sad outcome of the interrupted Renzler prosecution had made any lasting impression upon him.


After our return to Paris and in the months that followed, Montclaire diverted himself with other matters, most notably a close friendship with Mademoiselle Boudreau. And since that time, I have never known him to speak of the sad affair of Marie-Claire Bernard. Nor have I ever heard mention of the bowls. I supposed they were sold, perhaps to Monsieur Dulac and then to his German client after all, and now *The Tears of Buddha* have disappeared once more into the secretive world of private art collections.

# An Editor's Afterword

I hesitate to include possibly extraneous material in my account of the terrible murder of Marie-Claire Bernard. However, this clipping from the Roman daily *Avanti* came into my possession several years after the events of this case, and I believe it may have some bearing upon the story.

— Fitz

*Avanti. (Milan, October 2, 1910). Authorities in this north Italian city report that on Tuesday last a terrible discovery was made by the owner of a boarding house in the Naviglio Pavese canal district of the city. The naked corpse of a tall man with a large black moustache was found hanging from the ceiling light fixture in flat Number 3. According to the owner of the building, Signora Rivaldo, the flat had been rented a week earlier by a large man with a full black beard who appeared from his accent to be a Russian. He was accompanied by an associate, who spoke good Italian, but with a French accent.*

*Owing to the condition of the body, it was at first difficult to determine the identity of the deceased, but authorities have since learned that he was Egon Renzler, Third Secretary at the Austrian Embassy in Rome. According to the Polizia di Stato in Milan, Herr Renzler was in that city to attend a conference of olive growers and companies who export their olive oil to Austria.*

*Authorities in Milan have been circumspect about the matter, but Avanti's correspondent has learned that Herr Renzler's body was so badly mutilated, apparently by torture, that police suspect a madman is at large in the city. A Special Notice of Apprehension has been issued by the Carabinieri, warning citizens to be on watch for the large bearded Russian and his French companion.*